BROTHERS'
HAND

BROTHERS' HAND

MICHAEL J. SAHNO

Published by
SAHNO PUBLISHING
P. O. Box 46506
Tampa, FL 33646

First Edition
Printed in the United States of America

ISBN 978-1-944173-00-5

Library of Congress Control Number: 2015916578

Publisher's Cataloging-In-Publication Data
(Prepared by The Donohue Group, Inc.)

Names: Sahno, Michael J.
Title: Brothers' hand / Michael J. Sahno.
Description: First edition. | Tampa, FL : Sahno Publishing, [2015]
Identifiers: LCCN 2015916578 | ISBN 978-1-944173-00-5
Subjects: LCSH: Man-woman relationships--Fiction. | Amputees--
    Rehabilitation--Fiction. | Occupational therapists--Fiction. | LSD
    (Drug)--Psychological aspects--Fiction. | Hand--Wounds and injuries--
    Fiction. | Communities--New York (State)--Fiction.
Classification: LCC PS3619.A46 B76 2015 | DDC 813/.6--dc23

Cover Design by
Ryan Ratliff: RR Web and Print

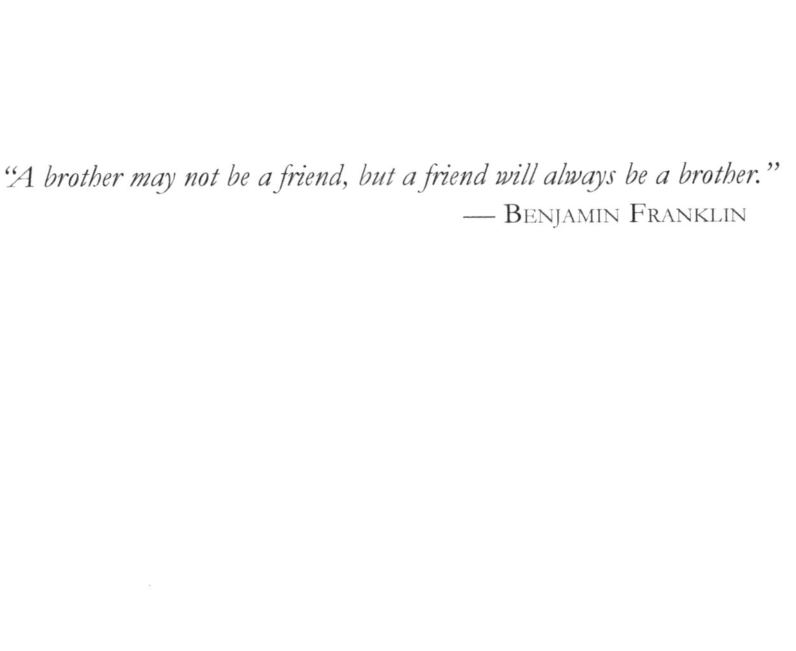

"A brother may not be a friend, but a friend will always be a brother."
— BENJAMIN FRANKLIN

PART
ONE

CHAPTER ONE

JOHNNY CARUSO THREW outrageous parties.

In the heart of Carverville, New York, six miles southwest of Elmira, stood a towering statue of Nathaniel Hawthorne. Regal and somber, his stony face looked down on an expanse of Bruford Park dotted with the blazing maples and sycamores of early October. Beyond, where the playground used to be, four blocks from the corner of Chestnut and Applewood, Macy's Market squatted like some meager testimonial to a bygone era. And by the market, at the end of Carriage Road, Johnny Caruso's house was alight with music and voices.

Inside, at the far end of the living room, among a clutter of empty glasses, beer bottles, and half-eaten bowls of chips, Jerome Brothers stood listening to the blue-eyed brunette in the leather jacket. Scarcely able to hear her above the metal roar of the stereo, he was painfully aware of the nearness of her body—although his twenty-eight years to her sixteen made her seem miles, lifetimes, away. But he continued to listen, smiling a little over his glasses as she prattled on about other parties, fights at the high school, and the Christmas shopping she'd already begun. She shifted without transition from topic to topic, as if she'd learned English from TV ads. To Jerome, her voice registered somewhere between a goat's bleating and a donkey's braying.

"Like, what a total dork!" she said. "Can you believe that?"

He shrugged. He had no idea who she meant. "What's that?"

"*Ronnie!* Jerry, man, aren't you even listening to me?"

"Mmhmmm," he said. "Go ahead."

"So *any*way...." On and on she went.

He drifted off again, making an effort to look attentive. These parties are sometimes a blessing and sometimes a curse. Guess I know which one this is....

He sipped his orange juice, wondering as he glanced around the room if there were anyone else there not drinking, or, for that matter, anyone else over the age of twenty-one. It seemed unlikely. Johnny Caruso's crowd was mostly high school kids—with a few freshmen and sophomores from Elmira College—but they were the most interesting and lively bunch Jerome knew. He thought of telling the girl how he'd lost touch with the old crowd when he'd gone to school in Pennsylvania to study political science. How he'd found most of his peers, there and afterward, intolerably boring. How before the age of thirty they were marrying and settling down, spending their earnings on condos and convertibles. He'd been to two parties with old friends, and both evenings had consisted of a tedious babble of Individual Retirement Accounts, tax shelters and CDs—*not* compact discs. They'd become self-absorbed, superficial: so practical, so financially solvent. So old.

This group, for all their wretched music and adolescent chatter, was alive. Even their cynicism was somehow innocent. At least they didn't talk about their kids, or their insurance policies.

The leather-jacket brunette prattled on, oblivious to the fact that she never quite commanded his attention. Gradually he became aware that, although her red miniskirt and dark hair stood in stark relief against the Carusos' off-white wall, a kind of blue halo glowed around her that had not been there before, as if she had some kind of magical aura, or had become radioactive. He blinked hard several times, and each blink revealed the blue silhouette of her body and of the corners of the room on the insides of his eyelids, blue neon lights in a coal-black sky.

A rush of adrenaline made him sit down, suddenly breathless.

"Are you okay?"

"I'm not sure."

"You're not gonna puke, are you?"

"No," he said, "I'm not drunk—something in my drink...." His stomach spasmed violently.

And then Johnny Caruso stood over him, curly blond hair in his eyes, grinning like some bizarre toothpaste ad. "Hey, dude!" he said, menacingly cheerful. "Just kickin' in, huh?"

Jerome blinked. The room blinked back, wavy. "What the hell did you put in my drink?"

"*Blue Dragon*, man." He gestured like a used-car salesman, proud of the merchandise. "Don't worry, man. It's good shit. *Real* clean. You're in for a good long ride. Wow, I'm surprised you got off so soon. It's only been like an hour since I dropped it in there."

Jerome was reeling. Blue and translucent green planets pulsed at the corners of his eyes, floating out of sight when he tried to focus.

Johnny laughed. "Check him out, man! He's buggin'!"

The leather-jacket brunette gave Johnny a shove. "You're an asshole. You don't just *put* that stuff in somebody's drink without telling him. Jesus!"

"Aw, come on, lighten up. He'll have a blast." He laughed, a little too loudly. "Right, Jer?"

"I can't believe you dosed me." He began to perspire. "Little bastard."

Johnny laughed again. "Fuckin' lightweight! That'll teach you to drink orange juice at my party." He grinned with fiendish pride.

"Jonathan," Johnny's mother's voice floated up from the basement, "what's going on up there?" She stayed downstairs every time he had a party, oblivious—or pretending to be—to the chaos above.

"Nothin', Louise. Just havin' a few laughs," he called back. Then, "Chill out, guys, I think she's comin' up soon."

The guys swallowed their smoke quickly, blowing it out onto the porch, lighting cigarettes in rapid succession to cover the sickly-sweet smell.

Jerome stood and headed for the porch. "I need some air," he said thickly. He sounded to himself like a record being played at a slow speed.

"Are you okay?" the brunette repeated, as if she had just arrived on the scene. Jerome did not answer.

"Hey, man, just enjoy the ride!" Johnny Caruso called.

Jerome headed out the door, polishing his glasses with the front of his denim shirt. The leather-jacket brunette's heels clicked behind him. He breathed the crisp autumn air, and the autumn seemed to breathe back, enveloping him in memories of his childhood: the first pew in church, his parents beside him prim and unmoving as mannequins. The choir sang a hymn, something vast and resonant. It rang from the marble, filling him with music and stained-glass visions. He sang with them in his mind, feeling as tall and proud as the priest. His scalp tingled with emotion. His heart lifted out of him, a sunlight serenade.

The leather-jacket brunette stood beside him now, quiet, as if somehow sharing in this moment she could not possibly touch. Nearly dusk, light gleamed on the railroad ties down the hill below the house. A light breeze blew, picking up the dry leaves and tossing them, swirling, across sidewalks and lawns. Above them, a sliver of moon hung in the sky like a fingernail clipping.

Just then Mrs. Caruso came out to feed the cat. "Herrrre, Maxine. Kittykittykitty. Oh!" She stopped. "Jerome and—Sandra, is it?"

The leather-jacket brunette made a slight curtsy, absurdly polite. "Yes, ma'am. How are you?" Her voice trembled.

Mrs. Caruso seemed to sigh a bit. "I'm all right. And how are you, Mr. Brothers? You look a bit woozy."

"I'm okay," he lied. "I just needed some air is all." He almost laughed. It sounded like he'd said "aerosol."

"Maxine!" crowed Mrs. Caruso. "Where is that damn cat? Excuse me," she said in apology for the curse. From above came a faint meow, and the three of them looked up. Jerome nearly burst into laughter at the sight of the big grey tabby in the maple tree beside them, way out of reach near the end of a small limb and almost invisible except for her face, bug-eyed and insistent. The tree perched on a grassy ledge at the back of the yard that led down to railroad tracks.

Mrs. Caruso folded her arms. "Well, I'll be darned. She's gotten herself stuck up there again." She turned abruptly toward the house. "John-NY!" she called.

Jerome and the leather-jacket brunette exchanged looks.

"Oh, I'm *sure* he can't hear me over that noise he calls music." She chuckled, as if embarrassed that she might have insulted them, too, in condemning her son's taste.

Jerome snapped from his reverie with a sudden and profound urge to climb the tree. "That's okay, Mrs. Caruso. I'll do it."

He felt completely lucid again, omniscient, although the yard around him expanded and shrank, breathing with an almost palpable life of its own. The task seemed important, predestined, as if he were the hero in some fifties movie—the stranger who pulls the young girl from the burning house, the substitute teacher who single-handedly rescues the class from kidnappers. Filled with excitement and determination, he imagined himself in the newspaper, holding the cat and smiling coolly while jealous firemen looked on in dismay. Preposterous, of course. He tried to shake the thought off, the way a wet dog shakes off rain.

"Oh, that isn't necessary," Mrs. Caruso said. "Besides —"

"No trouble at all," he said. He had not been up in a tree in so many years that the novelty, the hint of peril, offered sufficient incentive. "I'll climb the tree and get the cat," he told himself simply. "Climb tree, get cat. Tree, cat." It was absurdly obvious, as plain as the moon above. There was no stopping him.

"Oh my God," breathed the leather-jacket brunette.

"What's wrong, dear? Do you think he's too heavy for the branches?"

She hesitated. "Not exactly, no," she said. "It's just that he's a bit *old* for this sort of thing, you know?"

Mrs. Caruso nodded. "Well, that's all right, dear. I'm sure he'll be just fine." With that, she threw her scarf over her shoulder and went inside. The leather-jacket brunette followed.

The neighborhood spread before Jerome like a panoramic camera-shot from some old movie. For a moment his mind went blank. A caterpillar perched near him on a branch, inches from his face, huge, black and orange. He touched it, aware only of a slightly bristly feel as it tensed and fell, curling in midair, to the grass below. Cat, he thought, cat and caterpillar. The connection seemed obvious, profound, but its significance immediately flew away, lost in the cosmos with the Tao of strange sensations and active-contemplative perception, a universe of Isness and Suchness and Inner Light.

And suddenly he slipped, his left foot scraping away the piece of bark on the branch. Conscious only of the wheeling, tilting world of colors around him, mingling with the low sad note of the oncoming train, he fell earthward. He rolled down the short ledge, right beside the railroad ties, one arm slung across the metal track.

In a flash, the train bored down upon him like an unstoppable monster, and though he pulled his arm back at the last moment, the monster had him. He felt only a brief tug and undeniable pressure and then he was rolling away across the grass screaming. No pain came at first but the sense of loss struck immediately, its fury magnified a thousand times by the drug pulsing through him.

He woke from the dreamy cloud of acid but it came back, kaleidoscopic, wheeling on him. Ghoulish hallucinations, devil-faces, and myriads of barbed arrows bombarded from all directions. The sky heaved and churned, made him vomit bitterly with all of his strength. Blood poured from the end of his arm, spouting over him as he lay back, gasping. He closed his eyes tightly, green and purple and vermilion pinwheels spinning wildly behind his eyelids, and the sound of the train died away. He sobbed, his pulse booming like a cannon in some faraway valley.

CHAPTER TWO

ED ROBBINS LAY back on the couch, a bottle of Miller in one hand and a cigar in the other. Almost six o'clock. He picked up the remote, flipped on the TV with a pessimist's sigh, and settled himself among blue velour pillows.

Margaret would have been, should have been, home, but she was working overtime again. Obviously. It seemed unfair, having to wait for dinner like this, and he almost decided, right then and there, to get up and put a couple of TV dinners in the oven. But then he realized she would be reheating last night's beef stew, so he decided to just wait it out.

He'd had to do more than his share, most of his life—waiting for noon to come, so he could have a lunchtime beer or two, waiting his turn in the unemployment line—waiting, waiting, waiting. Waiting for a job offer that never came. He was sick of it: he had paid his dues, been a good provider, a damn good one. And still the endless waiting.

Now he waited for the news to begin, sure that it would, as always, be mostly bad: murders, plane crashes, the constant babble about toxic waste and the ozone layer and BTUs—things he didn't quite understand. And as always, no matter what kind of shitstorm was about to blast through Carverville, the monkeyish smiling weatherman drew grinning faces. Even on snow- and rain clouds.

And so, as if admitting he just lost an argument with the television, Ed settled back to absorb these trivial tragedies.

"Good evening, I'm Donald Fairmont, and this is Action News at six. A Carverville man has been hospitalized after a bizarre train accident that left him without his right hand, although he apparently sustained no other injuries. Twenty-eight-year-old Jerome Brothers of Carverville, a former political sci—"

A jolt of adrenalin rocked him. "Holy shit!" Ed rose like a shotput from his beery lethargy, groping for the phone, knocking cigar ashes on the end table and almost spilling his Miller. He dialed.

"—upon the scene, at the home of Louise Caruso of Carverville, during a party given by her son, eighteen-year-old John Caruso, a student at local Fillmore Leonard High. Jane?" The camera cut to a shot of a reporter standing outside the Caruso home.

"Thanks, Don," she said. "The conductor of the train, bound for Washington, D.C., did not appear to be aware of striking anyone, as the train never stopped. Brothers had been in a tree in the Carusos' backyard, which borders the railroad line, reportedly trying to rescue —"

"Goddamnit!" Ed yelled. There was no answer at his parents' house and he felt somehow obligated to talk about this freakish event, big news for Carverville, with someone else who had been watching the news, someone with whom he could, through the phone, share the adrenalin flow, exchange words of surprise and horror. He called the Carusos and got a wrong number, looked it up in the phonebook, called again. The line was predictably busy. He tried calling Margaret at work.

"Good evening, Arnold Corporation, this is Anne, how may I help you?"

"Extension three-one-o." Ed realized how out of breath he was, excited beyond alleviation now, as if Jerome had been his own son. He probably sounded like a very specific obscene phone caller. Extension 310 rang once, twice, three times.

"Human Resources, this is Danielle," chirped a bright young voice on the other end.

"Is Margaret there?"

"No, I'm sorry, she's left for the night. May I take a message and have her get back to you sometime tomorrow?"

"Do you know when she left?"

"Oh, about ten minutes ago, sir, you *just* missed her," she said as if she meant to sound comforting.

He took a swig from the bottle. "Okay, well, I guess she'll be here in about ten minutes, then. Thanks, anyway."

"No problem."

"Have a good n—"

She hung up before he could finish. He realized he was still breathless. He slugged the rest of his beer, slumped on the couch with a weary sigh, and stared at a television story about how crack had infiltrated small-town America.

"Shit," he said to the empty room.

CHAPTER THREE

THE RIDE TO the hospital made Jerome think of a movie scene where a man in an ambulance, after taking an overdose of some powerful hallucinogen, believes that writhing worms are literally streaming off of him. When that precise thing happened to Jerome, the EMTs strapped him into the stretcher to prevent him from hurling himself across the ambulance. He screamed and sobbed, raving that the worms were going to devour him—they seemed to be coming from inside his body—then cried for the lost hand, moaning, "My hand—the worms—my hand—train—worms…."

Mrs. Caruso, holding his good hand, was not amused.

She had watched while Jerome tried to retrieve the cat, saw the whole thing from her window. She had dialed 911, ventured out onto the dusty railroad tracks and picked up the severed hand—holding her breath, wincing, not looking at it—and sat by Jerome in silence on the way to the hospital, and before, when he sat, vacant eyed and moaning, waiting in shock for the ambulance. She was terrified when he came out of the shock, lurching forward in the stretcher and almost losing the wrapping around his arm. She knew only that he was delirious, and his babbling about worms frightened her.

When she was much younger, she had once seen a dead skunk filled with maggots by the roadside, and the image intruded suddenly in her mind. Aside from Jerome's lost hand, she had never in her life seen anything more horrible.

The hand sat now between them in a bucket of icepacks. She'd searched in vain for ice in the freezer—Johnny and his friends had used it to make screwdrivers—deciding at last to wrap it in paper towels. Putting the whole business in a bucket, she then covered it with packages of frozen vegetables—carrots, peas, green beans. "I hope this will do the trick," she'd muttered to herself, fighting the rising panic in her chest. After what seemed an eternity, the ambulance finally arrived, and she carried the bucket out to them, holding it in front of her like a potted plant. The EMTs provided icepacks, so she was sure the hand could be saved.

Had she not wrapped it in paper towels, the hand would almost certainly have been saved.

CHAPTER FOUR

MARIA SANTISIA ROSE from her bed like a cat uncurling in the sun. She stretched her arms above her head, palms flat, like someone in a temple—the "salutation to the sun," her yoga book called it—and then relaxed again, exhaling slowly and completely. She shook her mane of curly black hair back and forth, running a hand through it and yawning with comic exaggeration. Brr, it's cold in here, she thought.

Tossing back the covers, she leaped from the bed, landing on the shaggy maroon carpet like a gymnast. She stretched some more, moving quickly through a series of simple exercises, then knelt at the foot of the bed, palms on the floor in front of her in yet another yoga position, and prayed. She prayed for several minutes, her breath slow and deliberate, then arose with a faint smile and headed for the kitchen.

Her cat, Rasputin, awaited her at the door. "Hi, baby. Come on in," she said, as if he were an old and welcome friend arriving at an inconvenient moment. "I'll bet you're hungry, huh, kiddo? Yeah," she purred, and he purred back, nuzzling her leg.

"Mrow," said Rasputin.

"Mrow," Maria answered, her deadpan imitation flawless.

"Mrow," he repeated, looking at her with almost human annoyance. He circled her legs, meowing until she poured him food and fresh water, and handed it down to him.

Since she did not have to be at the hospital until ten, she took an extra long shower, lingered over her cereal—decorating it with blueberries as though preparing a treat for a small child—and read until it was nearly nine o' clock. The morning paper had not come yet, and she had to content herself with the previous day's medical section. She scanned for anything related to her work as an occupational therapist, but most of the newer discoveries seemed to have more to do with basic nutrition than surgery or physical therapy.

Finally, on the last page, she did find one interesting article concerning the growth of artificial organs. She nodded as she read, thinking that, without damaging the body's immune system, or being rejected by the other organs as transplants often were, this would be a revolutionary advance—if it were successful with human recipients. It might even be possible with prosthetics, she thought, whereby the patient would be temporarily able to replicate, like salamanders or starfish.

She remembered a lecture one of her professors had given in Anatomy and Physiology. "The immune system," he had said, "is a framework of elaborate intricacy, a delicate system, like a spider's web in fragility, and a computer in terms of efficacy. The body's ability to fight off various intruders—viruses, infections, and so forth—is directly proportionate to the strength of the immune system's *foundation*. In AIDS patients, for example, the injection of any bacillus could prove inevitably fatal, as the body's immunodeficiency would trick it into believing the intruder to be virtually harmless. In the case of the saturnine laboratory monkey—that is, a healthy specimen who is nonetheless unamused at his captivity —" here the students had laughed "— in his case, the immune system is, of course, *far* superior to that of the AIDS patient, and, in fact, almost equal to the healthy person, even superior to that of some—people who often eat at Burger Doodle, for example."

It's an interesting problem, Maria thought, and hoped that it would some day be resolvable.

CHAPTER FIVE

LOUISE CARUSO GAZED from her kitchen window onto the sunless lawn. Her mind comfortably blank for the moment, she enjoyed the view of grey-bright sky and autumn trees, burnt rusty orange by the season's slow unfolding. Somewhere deep within, however, her brain wrestled with something of great import and would not let go.

In the past two days, she'd been to the hospital three times to visit Jerome Brothers, who, though morose, had put on the brave show of the terminally stiff-upper-lipped: no mention of the hand, except one casual and ironic "just a scratch," and she had not known what to say. It felt a little like calling on someone just diagnosed with a malignant tumor, except that in Jerome's case, he would be alive a while yet. And anyway, she was sure the hand would be saved, even though the stump was wrapped in an appropriately small bandage.

She hadn't asked him about his "spell." There was no need.

He'd said, "Hope I didn't give you too much of a scare in the ambulance," and then he grinned. She could tell he didn't give a damn one way or the other, but conversation had to be made.

"Oh, no," she lied. "You were just upset, dear. Who could blame you?"

"I guess I was delirious. Doctors say I got a pretty good bump on the head." This was a baldfaced lie, but he simply could not bring himself to tell her the truth. How would she react if he told her that her precious Jonathan *dosed* him with acid? No way. A bump on the head, that's all. She probably hadn't even noticed the size of his pupils. Then again, what if she did? He'd tell her the whole goddamn thing if it came to that....

Mrs. Caruso hadn't noticed the size of Jerome's pupils nor did she question his bump-on-the-head fabrication. It struck her as perfectly reasonable that a person who had just fallen out of a tree and had his hand lopped off by a speeding locomotive should babble incoherently about worms, or about three-horned rhinos, for that matter. She saw nothing amiss, not in the accident, its climactic scene in the ambulance, or in his diminutive bandage. So, with peace in her heart, she stood idly in the clean and brightly-lit kitchen, noticing with mild discontent that the gauzy yellow curtains needed ironing and the glass in the storm window was slightly streaked. They would wait until tomorrow.

When she'd finished her tea and rinsed the cup, she put the cup in the dishwasher, which, being a newfangled item like the microwave, was something to adjust to, something to be handled with grave care and timidity, like a crystal vase. She meekly shut the cup within the vast tomb of the dishwasher, then stretched out on the overstuffed couch in the den, a little frowzy in her morning dress, and stared up at the only thing in the house that, aside from the poster-littered walls of Johnny's room, might be considered comparatively bizarre.

The print of the Yugoslavian painter Ivan Rabuzin's "My World"—"Moj svijet" painted into it in tiny letters—offered a bright portrait of a little country village perched atop a kind of orange bowl, over which towered huge and radiant sunflowers, indolently surreal, with a pale grey sky, cheery with deliberate cottonball clouds. It was a far cry from the Norman Rockwells and gaping crushed-velvet children one expected from a Louise Caruso. Even her closest friends had commented that the painting was, well, a "little odd," but she liked it all the same. Somewhere beneath her malt-shoppe reminiscences and *Reader's Digest* consciousness, she believed, hid something of a poetess.

But that tiny poetess was far away as she relaxed into the over-stuffed couch. She wondered if her cousin Margaret's husband, frumpy old Ed, had found work yet, and she decided to give them a call. Ed had been laid off since the spring, and as carpetlayers were in low demand in Carverville, he'd spent much of the summer, and on into the fall, fishing.

Ed had never been much of a breadwinner anyway, she recalled, preferring to call in sick as often as possible so that, as Margaret told it, she would often see his big shaggy head at the end of their hammock, immobile as a building, as she headed out to her own job. When he had a job, he took personal days by the score, often the consequence of a hangover, so money was even tighter for them than for most middle-aged couples. Margaret had become something of a nag since the layoff, he would say, while continually claiming he was trying to find "something halfway decent." Louise suspected he was dead drunk most days, gloomily frowning past his fishing pole over one lake after another.

She dialed the phone.

"Hello." It was Ed.

"Hello, is Margaret there, please?" She knew she wasn't, merely wanted Ed to acknowledge it, perhaps even reflect upon *why*.

"Nope, she ain't here. Can I take a message?"

"Ed, this is Louise."

"Cousin Louise?" He sounded surprised.

No, she thought, *Uncle* Louise. "Yes, it's me. How are you, Ed?" She formed the words with caution, as if he were a terminal patient, or perhaps a paranoid schizophrenic prone to sudden violent outbursts.

He sighed. "Oh, naht too bad. Hangin' in there."

"Any idea when Margaret will be back?"

A pause, as if he was calculating the hours. "Well, I'm naht too sure, Louise." Oh, you *wouldn't* be, she thought. "What's today, Tuesdee?"

"Yes, Tuesday. Tuesday the sixth." Louise was, of course, appalled that Margaret supported Ed, but she had vowed not to say anything to either of them. Ed's drinking was too sensitive a topic, after all, and certainly none of *her* affair.

Ed forcibly exhaled on the other end of the line—he was lighting a cigar. "Pffffh," he inhaled. "Yeah, Tuesdee—" he exhaled slowly "—Tuesdee she uzhee works late. So, 'bout six, six-terdee."

Louise sighed. "Well, would you tell her I called please, Ed? I should be home all night."

"Okey-doke," he said in a clipped tone, suddenly alert and almost business-like. "I'll have 'er give ya a call back after she makes dinner—prob'ly seven, seven-terdee, somewhere innair. Okay, love?"

She hated it when he called her that. "Okay, Ed," she managed, and then, with great effort, added, "Thanks very much. Take care, Ed."

After hanging up, Louise returned to the kitchen and looked out the window. The nerve of that monster! Here was Margaret, slaving away for him, and all he did was drink and fish and sleep, making half-hearted attempts to get another job...in fact, he probably wasn't even trying, just loafing around and scratching that frizzy head of his, while Margaret did everything for the both of them. It's downright sinful, she thought.

It had been one thing when he at least had a job: sure, they'd had their share of fights, especially when Ed stayed a little too late at the club and couldn't go—or just didn't want to go—to work the next day. That was one thing, but this—well, it was going on six months—or was it seven? It was just inexcusable.

And yet something made her envy Ed a little. Those pool-halls, where men talked about sports and work and women, talked and drank and sang songs (she thought), laughing raucously, seemed just a little bit exciting. She had never been inside a bar, of course. "Dens of iniquity," she always called them, just as her mother taught her. And like her mother, she had always been a near-tee-totaler, indulging only on special occasions, and then, in strict moderation, which was considered unusual for an Italian family, but acceptable on the Weatherbury side, of which Louise Caruso's mother was the family matron.

Then, too, her father had been known to stop at the local tavern once or twice a year, usually when he got his Christmas bonus, or on April Fools' Day, when he would come home with some foolish gag or other. He'd waltz in, just as serious as you please, whiskey on his breath and a gleam in his eye. And when he'd pull out two rubber snakes and make a face—"Aargh!"—the girls would scream as predicted, then laugh nervously behind their mother, while he roared with merriment.

"Bill Bagione!" her mother would say. "You're drunk."

"Drunk?" her father would exclaim, laughing. "I've never been drunk in my life! Just a couple of hot toddies with the boyos from the shop, dear." Then he would kiss her, gently, with a theatrical gesture, chucking her under the chin.

Yes, there was something marvelously seductive and mysterious about going to these dark places and letting go of all propriety, luxuriating the whole next day in the frail ennui and corruption of the day-long "morning after." But no, it was perfectly frightful, a sin that he, Ed, should be so completely, so—well, morally bankrupt, that's what it was. Just plain cruel and selfish. Something would have to be done.

CHAPTER SIX

MARIA STOOD AT the end of the supermarket checkout line, awaiting her turn. It was 4:15. In less than an hour she would meet with Jerome Brothers, a new patient who lost his right hand in "a train wreck," Dr. Fox had told her, and who was still in a bad state psychologically. He had been under the influence of LSD upon his arrival at Ford Memorial and, although apparently not actively delusional or in danger of a psychotic episode, his behavior had been somewhat erratic. In short, he'd treated the incident like a minor inconvenience, devoid of emotional colorings.

She reviewed these things calmly while the checkout line inched forward. She tried to picture him in her mind, this Jerome Brothers, so that she could give him the warmth and support he would need. It had been difficult to do that with some of her patients lately. After her divorce, an ugly affair that left her comfortable but somewhat broken up at twenty-eight, her natural kindness and firm but loving approach were almost becoming rote, a have-a-nice-day-please-come-again litany of motherly encouragement and coaching, like a speech from a bad movie script.

More than aware of the situation, Maria fought the odds in order to keep it genuine and spontaneous, but it was hard sometimes to detach herself, to keep from bringing her problems home. It made her feel a bit like a psychiatrist, although it was not yet a problem, she thought. On the other hand she'd been out walking late at night recently, quite often.

Her thoughts drifted to other things while an elderly man ahead of her slowly removed several cases of diet soda from his cart. She thought of her brother, and wondered how his new data entry job was working out. Then for some reason—possibly the elderly man's presence—the memory of a former patient back in Syracuse rose up before her.

His name was Elmer, and he'd had a terrible accident on his farm, but not a farm accident in the usual sense of the phrase, where a boy is injured by a tractor or the new farmhand falls into the grain bin. Although, as the old man told her, his own "fool carelessness" had been at the root of it: one of his horses, a bay, stood on his foot, crushing his brittle bones to dust and making pulp of the foot. The bay stood there "like a mountain," the old man said, his grey eyes losing light even in the bright hospital room as he leaned heavily on his walker. He had sighed deeply, pained by the loss and by its many ramifications, the loss of his ability to perform certain chores, the perhaps inevitable foreclosure on the farm, and the way the remains of the foot, as sure as summer cricketsongs, would ache in humid weather, warning him of approaching thunderstorms.

Empathy had turned to an overwhelming sympathy, and her eyes filled with tears, as if she were the old man's granddaughter. The smell of antiseptic seemed to smother her, and she excused herself, hurrying to the bathroom where she wept the tears of the bereaved. Several people on the staff speculated that her response was an effect of her recent divorce—and she had devoted herself to an unnatural amount of time sitting at home on the living room floor listening to old Joni Mitchell songs. But she had always liked late-night walks, as well as Joni Mitchell songs; it was just that she enjoyed them *alone* now.

Maria unloaded carrots and rice from her cart while the cashier rang up the old man's diet soda. Thinking again of her patient-to-be, she wondered what words of encouragement she could provide, especially since he'd been under the influence when he'd had the accident, and assuredly still grieved the loss of the hand.

Perhaps he would already be in the anger phase, which might mean verbal abuse. She took a deep breath, and sighed it out slowly, serenely resigned to accept, as always, whatever might happen.

When she arrived home, she found Rasputin perched atop the refrigerator, glaring down on her with his usual boldness. She stood on a chair, more amused than upset, and hauled him down, scolding. "You're a bad little boy, aren't you?"

Rasputin purred his approval and nuzzled her leg as she poured him fresh water and food. While he ate, she teased him by petting him on the back, watching with affection as he flicked his long tail back and forth, back arching down in discontent. She smiled and went into the living room to flip on the TV, hoping to catch the weather brief on public television before she left for the hospital. Instead, there sat Jon Ebsen on the *Profiles* show interviewing Philippe Alvarez, one of her favorite authors. Although she had to leave in ten minutes, she decided to listen as Alvarez discussed his work.

"I think," he said in his broad Latino accent, "that to a fair extent, I was influenced by the work of American authors—just ordinary people trying to *cope*, as you say, with extraordinary events. As they no doubt will try, yes?" He laughed, and Jon Ebsen laughed with him, falsely, like a game-show host.

Maria marveled at how charming and urbane Alvarez seemed, how politely he dealt with the utter plasticity of bald old Jon Ebsen without condescension. It was grand of him, that good humor, yet also a little disappointing to see how well groomed and professorial he was. An indefinable quality in his dark face and eyes, his keen razorwhite smile, made him powerfully seductive, and somehow it seemed wrong that he was not plainer, less refined: a poor Spanish farmhand bent double from years of grueling labor.

For night shifts, she usually arrived at the hospital by 4:45. It was nearly five when she pulled into the lot, but she felt none of the anxiety she'd experienced earlier. Relaxed, a little melancholy, she would meet Jerome Brothers with the cool professional ease that had always typified her work, and for that she felt gratitude.

Jerome was perched on the edge of the bed when she walked in. He held a copy of *The Lord of the Rings* in his left hand, the bandaged right arm resting lightly on his leg. The curious, relaxed pose struck her; she had expected him to be lying back under the covers, with his head also bandaged. Instead, he sat fully clothed and looked, except for his missing hand, like anything but a patient. He glanced up and smiled faintly when she said, "Mr. Brothers?"

"Hi. You must be Ms. Santisia." My God, she's beautiful.

"Please, Mr. Brothers, call me Maria. I hate that 'Mizz.'"

He grinned, boyish. "I'm sorry. I'm afraid my social skills are somewhat lacking. Forgive me?"

"You're forgiven." Her pure objectivity made his chest surge upward, then sink down into the regularity of disappointment.

"And please, Maria—it's Maria, right?"

"Yeees...."

"If I'm going to call you Maria, you have to call me by my first name. It's Jerome. My friends call me Jer, as in Jerry." This, as an afterthought.

"Okay, Jerome —"

Again his heart sank, a little more now.

"— I'm going to be working with you for several weeks, depending on how things go. Dr. Fox already told you about me, I suppose. So —"

"Only that there was a Ms. Santisia to be 'working with me,'" he interrupted. "You're not exactly what I'd pictured."

"Oh? What were you expecting?" She seemed on the verge of taking offense, perhaps bracing herself for some hideously sexist remark. But she smiled coolly.

"Someone much older. Unattractive. Blue hair, a little on the heavy side."

She laughed, in spite of herself, and her laughter lit up the room until he felt himself stir restlessly under his clothes. He was tempted to leap under the covers.

"Well, thank you, I think," she said. "Now, on the more serious side —" she interrupted herself—"You're reading *Lord of the Rings*, huh? How is it?"

"It's good. Very entertaining. I always said I didn't like this sort of thing, but I'd never actually *tried* this sort of thing. It's better than I thought—kinda like Philippe Alvarez."

"Oh, do you like him?"

"Well, I haven't read more than one of his books, but it was pretty good. You like that sort of stuff?"

"Absolutely, I think he's terrific. I saw him on TV today."

"Yeah, he's all right." He seemed to tire of the subject quickly. "Anyway," he continued, "it keeps my mind off of matters at hand—no pun intended."

She didn't know whether to laugh or not, and since he did not, she merely smiled. Strange, she thought, this sense of humor in a patient—usually they were sullen at first, even vicious, steeped in self-pity. Could he have passed directly into the acceptance phase this early? No, it was impossible. "Now really, Mr. Brothers— Jerome—you shouldn't —"

"Joke about it? Why the hell not? I mean, it's either laugh or cry, right? Besides, its not like I *like* it, but, y'know, it's also not like I lost a leg, or my whole arm, or my —" he searched for another example "— my *spleen* or some other vital organ."

She ignored the comic tone, composing herself. "Well," she began, "you have a point. But you will need someone to help you adjust to your situation as smoothly as possible. As I said before, we'll be working together for several weeks. I'll be helping you dress, and learn to write left-handed, and so on, for the time —"

"Helping me *dress*?"

"Yes." She blushed. "Just your *outer* clothes: buttons, shoelaces. I'll show you some techniques to keep all struggling to a minimum—writing, doing average, um, daily activities—shaving, all that sort of thing. And we'll combine that with a certain amount of counseling about other options for the future."

"Options," he repeated with a frown.

She hesitated. "Yes. Prosthetics, for example."

"Prosthetics."

"Yes. Artificial —"

"I know what they are," he said, without any discernible emotion whatever. "Forget it."

"Well, now, Mr. Br—"

"Absolutely not. I'm not going to walk around with a fucking mannequin hand for the rest of my life. Just call me 'Stumpy.'"

She looked at the floor. "Well, of course, you would have complete movement, all the newest technology —"

"Oh yeah!" He said it much too loudly, but he was smiling again. "Jerome Brothers, astronaut. A man barely alive." He lowered his voice, dramatically. "We can rebuild him. We can make him better than he was. Better..."

"Mr. Brothers —" she began.

"Stronger..."

"*Mr.* Brothers —"

"Faster! Dum dum DA dum —"

"Jerome!" she shouted, then reddened immediately. This man was too much. His sense of humor was sicker than that of most doctors. Was he insane? Dangerous? It seemed unlikely, but for an instant she was afraid to be alone with him.

"I'm sorry," he said. "I just *don't* respond to 'Mr. Brothers.' It's worse than being called 'sir.'"

She sighed, exasperated.

"Kinda like that 'Mizzz,'" he said, and they both laughed, she with lingering discomfort, he, more raucously than ever.

She began again. "There *are* other options."

"Options? Like what, a hook?" He laughed. "I can see me now: Captain 'The Hook' Brothers, king of the high seas. Why not just graft a garden tool onto the end of my arm? It dices, it slices...." He stopped abruptly, serious again.

It was like watching a character actor imitating Hollywood stars.

"Look," he said almost gently, quietly, "I'm sorry. I know I'm getting out of hand here, no pun intended. But it's *not that big a deal.* It's only one hand. Let's just forget the 'options' and concentrate on your therapy. Please."

His eyes told her he was sincere. "Okay. Maybe at another time we can discuss it, but for now —"

"You can discuss it," he said, grinning broadly. "But I *won't listen!*" And he laughed a little laugh in the back of his throat.

CHAPTER SEVEN

HE'D GROWN UP in Carverville, New York. Born in Johnson City, orphaned at the age of seven months, raised by his aunt and uncle, who moved him to Carverville when he was four years old. Although he never knew his real parents, he had no reason to think of Jake and Laura as anything but, except that they told him about his parents' accident when he was quite young. In a strange way, the accident seemed appropriate to him, a gift of Providence, as Jake and Laura had been unable to conceive a child. Now they had one, although the price had been great.

Jerome remembered little of Johnson City, and life, it seemed to him, had not officially begun until the three of them—Jake in his greatcoat and Laura bundled like a babushka, holding the four-year-old Jerome in her arms like a Christmas package—piled into the old station wagon and headed west toward Carverville, a little town nestled in the woods between Big Flats and Wellsburg, just over the line from Pennsylvania.

The deaths of John and Mary Brothers had been surrounded by only superficially ordinary circumstances. The couple, married less than two years, left their beautiful boy alone with a sitter for the first time in seven months. John—his big six-foot frame swathed in the heavy brown overcoat Mary's parents bought him for Christmas, black hair slicked back, shaven and smelling of Old Spice—walked Mary out to their clean, blue '59 Chevy, rapt, smiling down on her piled-up blonde hair. The Chevy had just had new brakes put in, and had been washed and waxed, and he felt a proud, warm surge of benevolence as he escorted his wife to her side of the car.

They were going out for dinner, and to a club for dancing, without the dubious benefit of another couple's company. And so they said goodbye to the babysitter—Mary rushing around with last minute instructions, trebly-repeated, until John winked and smirked and rolled his eyes, ruefully amused by the "mother-hen" side she'd sworn never to assimilate.

The babysitter listened tolerantly, smiling and saying, "Yes ma'am," over and over, like a mantra.

And then they were gone, vanished forever into the crisp January night.

Mary Brothers stepped into the dim light of the Carriage House Restaurant, prepared to have what would be her last meal. The baby had become the center of her universe in the past year-and-a-quarter, taking priority over all else. John had borne the load lightly, playing the role of father to the hilt: all the old clichés, from a handpainted antique of a wooden crib to "It's a boy!" cigars trotted out like ponies at a summer fair. Uncomfortable with the role, he had taken to smoking a pipe half-humorously, stylishly homely in the manner of the age, an archetype of "Dad," of all Dads. His youth was over, he felt deeply now, and soon, he thought, there would come an endless procession of Little League games, PTA meetings, teeth to be pulled, scraped knees to bandage and shoes to tie, and for every small advance that the boy made, for every tiny shining independence the child asserted, a little of John's heart would go with him, soaring away on the string of a paper kite.

Outside the Carriage House restaurant, above the distant mountains, a searchlight swept the cloudy sky. John stepped from the car, which he parked after letting Mary out at the door, and breathed steam out into the January night. Hands in pockets, he walked smiling across the cold smooth parking lot. He was happy.

Inside, John and Mary had little to say: it was enough, one could see, that they were together. They talked vaguely about the future over their prime rib and glasses of port wine, and Mary called the babysitter twice. And after a night of dancing to Chubby Checker and Little Richard records, they left for home.

The police would later discover that Joey Catalina, who had fixed the Chevy's brakes, had been at the dance hall that night. But no connection had been made, beyond the accusatory mutterings of several neighbors; there had been no apparent motive. The Chevy simply swung out onto the steep winding hill that led into Johnson City, and, having lost its brakes somewhere along the line, careened into a huge maple on the other side of a fence at the bottom of the mountain. John and Mary were killed instantly, but the whispered suspicion that the brakeline had been cut died after a few days—no investigation was ever made.

So Jerome, orphaned at seven months and barely cognizant of his parents' existence, had been raised by his aunt and uncle. And though they never moved from Carverville, the loss of his parents was perhaps responsible for a certain sense of rootlessness he carried with him, a feeling of not having a home even in the house to which, as a grown man, he returned with an ever-growing feeling of strangeness, like a foreign exchange student visiting an American family.

He had been a good student, but not an excellent one. In high school, not inclined toward athletics, he was more of a "pothead" than anything else, a closet intellectual who fancied himself quite enlightened from having read John Stuart Mill, *The Federalist Papers*, and the works of Marx and Engels, although he scarcely understood them.

College was different. He worked his way through Penn State and, although always most liberally assured that his well-rounded education, decorated as it was with an understanding of history and of the classics, would hold him in good stead and impress future employers, he soon found the reality quite different. In fact, upon returning to Carverville, he found himself working for a temporary agency (one of many), all of which he ultimately concluded to be a blight, an infestation of termites in the dilapidated house of The System.

Between working various short-term assignments as a junior accountant, one agency in particular called and offered a part-time job as a warehouse picker or stockboy, and the best thing they were ever able to come up with for him was a month-long stint as a loan review clerk at a corporation called the Shenandoah Mortgage Company. There, he learned about tax records and escrow waivers, disbursement authorizations, truth-in-lending disclosures, and countless other documents filled with pompous mumbo-jumbo he termed "legalese." And there, he had become employed long-term before his life was rudely interrupted by the accident that cost him his hand.

But the job had been even more mindnumbingly dull than it sounded, especially after the recent excitement of school. Far removed from the vagaries of his small town alma mater's alumni, free to begin anew with a willfully created and aggressively political identity, he became a partygoer, spending considerable time with those in college primarily to have a "good time," but not partaking of their Bacchanalian activities.

"No, thanks, I'm all set," he'd grin, holding up one hand in a faintly protesting way before whatever sweaty hand offered him a can of Piel's or Milwaukee's Best, quietly glorying in the private hilarity of others' growing intoxication. And yet, though no one minded his relative sobriety, it made him something of an emotional outcast. The night went on forever, the moon waxing and waning outside, while the same songs played again and again, and the voices grew hoarse and insistent. The room suddenly seemed to move rapidly away, leaving him alone in the crowd: an outsider looking at a party from a solitary corner, observer and not participant.

That sensation returned periodically at parties, at the Caruso house and elsewhere, and sometimes even at the office during lunch hour. He found himself suddenly swallowing an inexplicable rising fear, a surge that made him feel as though he were being carried out of himself, the direct converse of what he'd felt upon meeting Maria Santisia.

That had been a strange feeling, he remembered, as if someone had just turned the light on for him, as if he'd been living in semi-darkness up until this single moment of epiphany, the beginning of a fascination which would gradually sweeten before it could sour. He remembered telling her what he would later discover she'd already known: that he'd been on an acid trip at the time of his accident.

"Oh, they didn't tell you they put me in the psych ward when I first came in?"

She arched an eyebrow. "Noooo...."

"I got dosed. It was a teenybopper party, but I got dosed."

"What do you mean?" she asked, revealing in an instant a naïveté he could not help but find appealing.

"Someone put acid in my drink." He left Johnny's identity out of it intentionally, preferring to keep it private, for he was willing to forgive that cruelest of sick pranks. Not that Maria would know the difference.

"Is that so?" She looked amazed. "Well, they didn't keep you *there* long, anyway, right?"

"No no, only a few hours. A bad trip is difficult to shake yourself out of. And the psych ward is probably one of the three worst places I can think of to do it!"

"What are the other two?"

"Cleveland and Detroit."

They both laughed.

"So was it pretty awful?"

"It was for a while. But I came down to earth when this old drunk started talking to me. The guy was definitely a full-goose-bozo loony bird, you know?"

She smiled sidelong with her eyes.

"And apparently he was a hobo for quite a number of years, during the Depression and after. He told me these crazy stories about bumming around the country: like he hitchhiked to Florida with one of his buddies when they were pretty young, I guess—the kid's father left a house down there after the market crash—and when they get there, lo and behold, the house really is deserted. There's no running water, holes in the roof—it was a place to crash on the floor, you know? Anyway, they're really disappointed about the water situation, because they only had one bar of soap, and now there's no way to take even a shower. You can imagine how grungy two drunk hitchhikers who've been on the road for days would be."

Maria grimaced.

"So they're sitting there, totally dejected, when all of a sudden they get this little rain shower. And the guy—the one who was telling the story—runs outside with the soap and starts to undress right in front of the house."

"Oh, no."

"Oh, yes. And there was this little old lady watching from her living room window across the street, totally horrified. This guy stripped down to his underwear—which, of course, he described for me, right down to the tiger stripes —"

Maria began to laugh at this.

"— and he starts soaping himself up right there on the front lawn. His friend sits there, taking it all in, shaking his head, when the sunshower stops as quickly as it started. So there this guy is, soap in his eyes and ears, standing in a yard, his buddy laughing like hell at him, and this little old lady staring in complete disgust. He looks up, stretches his arms out and says, 'Come on, God, gimme one good one!' And *bang-o*! Rain shower number two."

"No way."

"Way! Not only that, but the lady across the street just about flipped, he said. She saw the whole thing, and the guy saw her reaction when the second shower hit: she just about lost her dentures, I guess. Can you imagine?"

"That is strange. But how did this guy's story get you off a bad LSD trip? I don't understand that at all."

"Well, I don't either, really, but I think it was partly because I was the 'new guy' on the ward, and partly because it was so totally *stupid*, but—I don't know, the way he told it—you really had to be there, I guess. I just *had* to pay attention, and it got my mind off all the craziness. I just laughed so hard—it was weeeird. And then, about three hours later, they come and check on me, and I'm okay—or I *acted* okay, at any rate. And here I am."

"You certainly don't seem psychotic to me. In fact, I thought you were a little off at first, but now I think I know you a little better. It's that sense of humor."

"You like my sense of humor, huh?"

"Yeah! I love it," she said, too effusively.

He arched an eyebrow. "Well, don't get used to it. I'm very difficult to get along with."

"Oh, come on now. You're easy to get along with. You're so nice all the time—at least with me. You should see *some* of my patients."

He smiled. "You've never seen me angry."

Maria smiled. "I think I have."

"When?"

She shrugged. "Oh, when I first met you. I think you were understandably angry about your situation—I remember a comment about Captain Hook...?"

"Oh. That. Well, I was just trying to lighten things up a bit. You were so damn serious and business-like."

Her jaw fell. "I was not!" She looked offended. "I was quite nice, I thought."

"We-ell..."

"Oh, come on. I was nice." Something about her protest repelled him slightly, as though she was idly flirting, but not with her heart. And again he felt that sinking sensation and a kind of longing. Weariness and boredom uncoiled around him like a snake.

He remembered what it had been like for him with other women. Into his relations would inevitably come one of two things: a kind of filial warmth, vaguely satisfying but sexless, devoid of the danger of eroticism; or an instant glow, followed by a fencing match of repartee and thinly-disguised coquetry, building his ego into a skyscraper of self-confidence, poise, strength. This with Maria was a fleeting dream. Though he'd felt something at the outset, it quickly degenerated into the brotherly/sisterly thing he half-hoped, half-feared, it would become.

She watched him, awaiting an answer.

"Well," he said. "I suppose you were nice. Cool. Professional. Detached." A pause. "But nice," he added with emphasis.

The irony was too subtle; attempts at wit were dying.

"Cool? Detached?" The sisterly, platonic nature of their acquaintance seemed firmly cemented, as if some valve between them had been shut off with a groan and click. "I thought I was so sweet to you," she said, but he was no longer fully engaged in the conversation.

"You were, you were," he insisted. It's over, no doubt about it. Maybe it never existed. Well. That's all right. We only have to work together for a few weeks. Never see her again after that. Time heals. Least I didn't get *too* close.

"...And you were so strange," she was saying, "so much different from my other patients."

Yes, that's what he was: her patient. A bug under a glass.

"There's something different about you. Your strength. You just acted like it was no big deal at first."

"Sure. Just a flesh wound. A minor, lifestyle-altering inconvenience." He smiled faintly.

Maria laughed. "I like you, Jerome. You're funny." She smiled with incredible warmth, and the strong barrier between them suddenly crumpled. He felt it hit him, this love he did not want, had already renounced, rising up in utter defiance.

"I like you too," he said, and the moment was thankfully gone. He shut it off like anyone with years of practice, tossing up an impregnable fortress with the utter nonchalance of clicking off a television by remote control, comfortable with the familiar horizontal line fading neatly to a pinpoint of light in a sea of black.

For now, they were just strangers. At least, they had just met, and had not gotten off to an amazingly good start. But he interested her, and when she left his room that first night, Maria had neither gone straight home nor on to her next client.

Instead, notebook in hand, she went to the nurses' station to get more information on Jerome Brothers. So far, all she knew was that he was attractive, tall and slender with glasses and sandy brown hair, green eyes—it struck her as odd that she'd noticed all these things in such a particular way—and a small "beauty mark" on his jawline, almost indistinguishable among his two days' growth of whiskers.

At the nurses' station, they gave her nothing more than the simple statistics she expected: height, 5'11"; weight, 165; DOB, 7/4/69.

"The Fourth of July," she mused. "That's funny."

The rest was nothing—a medical history devoid of anything other than his tonsils being removed and a fractured wrist. She gave the nurse a perfunctory "thank you" before moving on in silence.

CHAPTER EIGHT

JOHNNY CARUSO HUNKERED down on the bedroom floor between his stereo speakers. He had a Machetes and Begonias CD on, very loud, and words filled the room:

> *...So I tied off, baby,*
> *Wouldn't ya like to try it too?*
> *'Cause there's a whole lotta flashin'*
> *When the brown horse is crashin'*
> *Through your brain like a Subaru....*

He knocked his knees together, wagging his head up and down like a terrier. Bizarre images and lyrics filled his head most of the time, but tonight, the rush of furious drums and high-speed hammer-on guitar notes flowed through his dusty brain almost unnoticed. He was distracted, thinking about what he had done in spiking Jerome Brothers' drink with LSD.

Brothers was his neighbor, ten years his senior, and *might kick his ass*. But no, he thought, he wouldn't try it—too straight, too afraid of cops. Besides, it wasn't like Johnny was responsible for the *accident*. Everyone knew that the train came by at ten to five, and anyway, who in their right mind would climb a tree, by the tracks, at that time?

"Fuckin' cat," he muttered.

He had heard that people could flip out completely and wind up institutionalized after being dosed, but the notion seemed absurd. He had, himself, started with shots and beers, and the occasional joint or two, at nine, and now, twice that age, he'd progressed into a state of regular and varied drug use. Among his small cadre of renegade bikers and skinheads his ability to guzzle 151-proof rum was legendary, and his consumption of LSD in doses of up to 5,000 micrograms was considered laudable.

Now he crouched, as was his habit, between his speakers, tiny synapses sizzling and crackling in his brain. He wondered if he should send Jerome Brothers a card. He decided against it.

CHAPTER NINE

WHEN SHE HAD finished her preliminaries and bade him goodnight on that first day, Maria—promising to be back that Thursday—left Jerome alone in the hospital room, his roommate having checked out forever earlier that day. It had been kind of exciting, having someone die right next to him, especially with no emotional ties to consider or grieving relatives to console. The man had an aneurysm, the doctor had told him, so it was quick, and not necessarily painful. But Jerome knew it had been a bad way to go, the man's growl of "Aiiigh" startling him out of his Tolkien-spun reverie.

He tried now to return to that fantasy world, but the words were like hieroglyphics, remnants of some long dead language. Maria filled his mind: her eyes, her voice, the fact that she actually enjoyed reading, and mostly, her obvious determination to help him. He sat back in bed, looking out his window at the autumn trees, changed now to pale yellows, blazing reds, dull rust browns.

Something he'd read in college about "the great primal joke of the undignified nature of the human body" occurred to him, and he arched an eyebrow at his bedpan. The expression seemed true after all. There was not a shred of dignity to it all, he thought, no sense of sanctity about the body: it was a cruel joke of chance, just as the philosophers would have it, incontrovertible as the past.

Perhaps, he thought, in another age it had been different, but now the flesh was a trap, and bodily functions, indignities. It was obscene, somehow, like the passionate embrace of a lovestruck couple would be obscene if captured for posterity on thirty-eight millimeter. And the lost hand, the stump of an arm now bandaged to cover it, was final evidence. Like a fig leaf or an eyepatch, it served only to draw more attention to that which it purported to conceal.

So that was it. Fate had played a merry trick on him, first making him, like other people, subject to strange whims and urges, a prisoner of emotions and unattainable desires. Then it had taken his right hand, which, although he had always taken it for granted, seemed now to represent all of his power and masculinity.

As a boy, he remembered he had a disturbing tendency to get an erection at "inappropriate" moments. Once, in the third grade, it happened before school started, a result of the warmth of the radiator he leaned against as he looked out a window at the early-morning frost. Nothing could have been more innocent.

But Jenny Peterson saw him leaning forward, oppressively tumescent, and had pointed, looking both amused and aghast: "Jerry's got a hardon."

He'd blushed to the roots of his hair, he remembered, filled with shame and anger at the cruel prank nature played on him, and he'd turned abruptly back toward the window, wanting to disappear, pushing down on the front of his pants with both hands, trying in vain to make the aching organ subside. "JERRY WANTS TO MAKE BABIES WITH JENNY" was soon written on the bathroom wall, which was enough to make Jenny loathe him, and certainly enough to make him frightened of her power. More than anything, though, even more than shame and anger, it made him fascinated by the steady, vibrant heat of the radiator.

Embarrassed by the memory, a long-buried guilt rose in him, and he blushed as he had when he was ten. There was nothing wrong with him, he knew—it was perfectly natural, just as all these years later he felt the inevitable stirring with Maria. Yes, it was perfectly natural, and yet that was the whole problem: nature.

A priest he heard once described lust as associated with the Fall From Innocence, but Jerome thought that absurd. If anything, it was innocent to be aroused with so little external stimuli, whereas an adult man would most likely require something supremely erotic, voluptuous, or pornographic, to be so inspired.

Yet there was something to the priest's argument, some hazy connection among lust and copulation and other bodily functions, secretion, urination, defecation; somehow all tied up with that business of the "undignified nature of the human body." He sighed.

Before he went to sleep that night, he read just past the halfway mark in *Lord of the Rings*, then washed up, brushed his teeth—amazed at how quickly he was adjusting to doing these things lefthanded—and settled back into bed. They would be moving a new patient into the room tomorrow, he'd been told, but for now he was grateful for a night of solitude.

Still preoccupied with his earlier thoughts, he began to brood again. Like a child fascinated with the way his elbows and knees bend back and forth, he experimented with the muscles of his body, tensing his foot muscles, relaxing them, curling and straightening his toes, the slight effort making blood sing in his ears. Moving upward, he flexed each leg muscle, arms, neck and chest, flexing and unflexing until, relaxed and breathing evenly, he drifted toward sleep.

It would not come. Something kept him floating along, buoyed by some hymn to consciousness. Sleep hovered at the edges of his bed like the hospital curtain employed before an enema or some other medical invasion. A thousand thoughts and images rose up in his mind, the mutterings of a fatigued brain: snatches of description from Tolkien, lyrics of well-loved songs, questions, memories, babbling up in a muddled chorus.

"My life sucks," he whispered aloud.

The sound of his own voice in the darkness startled him. If he could believe in a reason for all this, it might not seem so bad, he thought. *If there was a God, He wouldn't let this happen to me without some purpose.*

There isn't, though, he thought, and felt his heart beat in his chest: and yet, and yet…. Finally, with a clumsy, painful self-consciousness, he said what, for him, was a prayer. "If there's anybody up there, if you can hear me, I want you to know I'm pretty damned pissed off, and I want some help."

His breathing slowed, and before the moonlight seeped in again through the blinds on his window, he was asleep.

But the night was not peaceful. He had a dream, morbidly vivid, that he was floating—a breathtaking, magical dream, like something from a childhood fantasy. First he floated over a farm, cornfield stubble and the round eye of a silo beneath him, then spots of black and whitish browns—cows, or horses, he couldn't be sure which. He drifted down toward them with a slow animal grace, no sound in his ears, as if in a vacuum and the canopy of sky above his parachute.

Without warning, he heard his name called loudly, and when he turned to look, he lost his ability to float and fell, crashing to earth with a sickening thud. At the moment of impact he landed on some huge blade that severed his arm at the elbow, and as he started awake, bolting upright in the bed, he grabbed onto the arm with his left hand, gasping. The same arm as in the dream. He panted, blood pounding in his temples, and in the injured arm, his heart racing.

He buzzed for the nurse, pleaded with her in a strident voice for painkillers. She gave him Demerol.

CHAPTER TEN

My boys be bay-id
My boys be flah,
And none of 'em nevuh
Wantsta weah no tah...!

THE BLARING RAP song, thumping out of the rolled-down window of a parked Pontiac, accosted Bill McCullough as he stepped into the sharp October wind. Fear gripped his chest in time with the heavy bass beat booming down on Carverville like Judgment Day. Bill slowed his breathing intentionally, pain rising in his sternum. He passed into the street.

A shabby looking boy and his mother, unkempt in her cornflower dress, went by, the boy looking tired, jaded beyond repair at seven. Huge strips of misshapen clouds swam in the sky like hammerhead sharks, and as Bill walked along he overheard a woman behind him say, in a downstate accent, "I *love* animal shows, you know? Except when they have insects. Give me anything but bugs. *Uf,* they just make me *itchy,* you know?"

Bill was drifting back in time to a place he did not care to remember. He'd been twenty-six years old, married for seven years to his first wife, Janice. She'd been his high school sweetheart. He'd inherited his father's lumber business and decided to settle in Johnson City with Janice, although he wanted to move west—Oregon, maybe, or even California, where, he had heard, the sun shone every day, the whole year through. But he'd settled instead, he and Janice, and now he had responsibilities. Things were a little tight at first, with the birth of their first and only son, but they got more manageable as time wore on. The lumber business settled into a fairly regular routine of tasks that Bill was able to master.

And then something terrible happened, something so intolerable that it shook his world apart, shook the foundation of his marriage until it, too, crumbled, making his whole life a wall from which bounced an endless and insinuating echo. Something he could neither accept nor absolve.

The memory reared up in him now with its cold implacable quality. He walked across the parking lot to his car, trying to quell it in vain as it whispered to him insistently from across the span of sixteen years.

He was twenty-six then. It was October twenty-seventh. Yes, that was why it gnawed him again; it was October, blackest month of all. He had just come home from work. Janice was out shopping. He walked into the den, flicking on the light as he went.

"Joey?"

No answer.

"Must be upstairs."

He went up to his bedroom, a small room at the opposite end of the hall from his son's room. "Joey?" he called again. Just before he reached his bedroom door he heard the response.

"I'm in here, Daddy."

Pushing open the door, he found Joey standing before the bureau, the top drawer open, the drawer he kept his personal things in. Joey stood before it with the .45 pressed against his small blond head.

He froze. "*Joey.*"

"Look, Daddy," he said, and before Bill could move or breathe or cry, he pulled the trigger.

Only then could he move, leap, in a furious terror and anger and disbelief screaming across the room, upon the boy, who crumpled beneath the smoke like a marionette and whose blood sprayed, scattered, along the wall, irrevocable, shockingly red. And he was still there clutching the ruined child, the ragged skull and frail cool body, choking and whispering out his litany of disbelief when his wife came home and found them.

Sixteen years ago, he said to himself. He leaned back against the cold vinyl seat of the Olds and lit a perfecto. A long, long time ago. He had sat like a man of stone at the funeral, at the divorce proceedings and after, coolly and furiously immobile, expression-less. And he had never spoken of it, except once, when he and Janice had their final shouting match. But never again after that, not to his parents, not to a priest, not to anyone.

And so it just flitted through him when it wanted (*Look daddy Look daddy*), swirling up and out of him. He would grip the steering wheel of his car, like now, or the sides of his armchair, or simply break out in a cold sweat and ride it out. But it was okay. That was a long time ago, and he had forgiven himself. He was sure of that.

He started up the car and pulled out into the street. They were going to be playing cards with the Robbinses tonight. That would be good. He looked at the sky, surprised at how dark it had already grown—the days getting shorter. October, blackest month of the year.

CHAPTER ELEVEN

THE DAY WAS clear and crisp, the sky bright as summer, and sunshine rang down on them like a bell. Three birds wheeled across the sky, black specks in the cool blue air. Breathing deeply, Margaret Robbins walked beside her husband.

They'd come to the park every Sunday when they were first married, but this was their first time in too many years. It had been different then, she saw keenly. Now this frizzy-headed frumpy man, with his potbelly and his dour face, was a stranger to her.

Ed liked to fish and watch football; she liked theater and art shows. He drank cheap beer in quantity; she settled for an occasional glass of sherry. The more she looked at him, the more she heard his wheezing sighs and felt his big arm beneath her hand, the more she thought she could blast him to kingdom come with a shotgun and keep a smile on her face before, during, and after. She acknowledged this silently, almost calmly, as a pregnant mother acknowledges the fact of the life within her. Yes, she despised him, as she would an iron chain around her ankles. More, since she had chosen him.

Two birds chirruped in a tree just beyond them, shattering the quiet murmur of the autumn breeze. For it was autumn now, every tree ablaze in reddish orange, purplish red, sun bright yellow, all towering above them in garish contrast to the stately and sedate deep green of the occasional fir and spruce.

Margaret sighed, remembering the spring after their first anniversary when she'd been a big-eyed brunette in snowy wool turtleneck and chamois navy skirt, alive and hopelessly young in Paris.

She remembered, walked again in her mind, the Champs-Elysée, Le Jardin du Luxembourg, the glorious Louvre with paintings by Dürer, Vermeer, Fra Angelico. And she saw them all crumble, each memory fading, as she glanced sideways at the dour old boy beside her. Old? She could not believe it had never occurred to her before. He had gotten old and dull, musty, while her life began at forty. How she had ever gotten him through the Louvre was beyond her now.

She looked over at him again, wondered what, if anything, he was thinking. "Do you remember when we were in Paris?"

"Huh?" He sounded dull, peevish.

"Do you remember when we were in Paris?" she repeated. "The summer after our first anniversary?" It had been spring, of course, but she remembered it as summer from having been overdressed for the weather.

"Yeh, yeh. Paris was nice." It sounded mechanical. Devoid of the nostalgia Margaret so cherished.

"It was beautiful," she said. "All those little shops, and the quaint little streets and cafes. And remember the Louvre? And the Eiffel Tower, oh."

He grunted. "Hmph. Eiffel Tower." He puffed his cigarette, inhaling sharply. It stuck straight out of the side of his mouth, a Bogart parody. "Yeah, dat was alright."

"Ed," she said, turning abruptly, "when are you going to get a jahb?"

"Cripe, Margie, I don't know." It was nearly a whine. "Somethin'll come up. Chrissakes, it's on'y been a few months."

"Six, Ed. Nearly seven."

He sneered. "But who's counting, huh? Jeezus, don't belabor it. I feel lousy enough about it as it is."

"Well," she said. That was all.

And they walked on as leaves fell slowly around them.

CHAPTER TWELVE

THE DOCTORS REQUIRED Jerome to stay at Ford Memorial a full week after the accident. He was still struggling beneath the weight of car loans taken out on old heaps that had become inoperable before the loans were fully paid off, and cost-of-living expenses that exceeded his income. Medical insurance and dental insurance had transitioned from rights to privileges—privileges to which he was no longer accustomed.

Without insurance, he was forced to go on disability. The only way to pay for the hospital services, as it turned out, was in small increments, and even in these circumstances the prospect of a bleak financial future loomed.

His initial responses to Maria's suggestions had been largely automatic: "*I* can do that," he would say before attempting to open packets of sugar for his coffee or pry the lid from a bland cup of tapioca pudding. She stood and watched as he struggled, until, cursing under his breath, he surrendered with an impatient sigh, and the inevitable question, "All right, what do I do?"

She brought in a vast array of everyday items, modified, or created especially for, people with a nonfunctional or missing hand. She brought him a dinner plate with a raised lip around half of its outer edge, so that he could push pieces of food across the plate without having to chase them. There were special utensils, like a "rocker knife" that had a curved blade and could be used by itself to cut food. And there were special gadgets for putting on socks, tying shoelaces, buttoning buttons.

She brought many of these, showing him a catalogue of similar items, and ordered the ones he requested. Then, having been called by a local agency to manage his case, she assumed full responsibility for assessing his home for modifications, and for continuing to act as his therapist. In the meantime, the first actual sessions of therapy began not long before he was to be discharged. Accepting help was not as difficult as Jerome expected, and he found himself grateful for it. He still keenly felt the painful self-consciousness and self-pity of the newly disabled, but his resolve to keep it to himself overpowered any impulse to complain.

Yet brushing his teeth remained a chore—setting the brush down on the sink, squeezing toothpaste carefully onto it, then picking up the brush with one swift semi-dexterous movement. And shaving, never one of his favorite rituals, was now a nightmare, so much so that he bought an electric shaver as soon as possible upon his release.

One Saturday afternoon, after he had gone through the daily basics of washing, dressing and shaving, Maria arrived. The day's plan was to teach him to print with his left hand. Outside, the sun was going down, light streaming in through the window, washing the room in a warm orange glow.

She guided his hand through the three separate lines of a capital *A*. They had just finished the lower case alphabet. "There you are," she said. "Just concentrate on forming the letters. Neatness doesn't count."

"This is unbelievable. I feel like a baby—couldn't I just make an X for my signature from now on? I don't do much writing other than signing checks, you know."

She smiled. "No, no, Mr. Brothers. We must learn to write all over again. This is an essential part of your recovery."

"Hey, what's with this 'Mr. Brothers' crap? It's —"

"I'm sorry," she said, blushing deeply. "It's Jerome. I forgot."

"Jerry."

She smiled. "Jerry."

"I'm crushed."

"Now, Mr. Br—"

"Ah —!"

"—Jerry, no flirting with the therapist."

"Was I flirting? I'm sorry. I thought all I said was 'I'm crushed.'"

"That's all you did say." She guided him through the letter *B*. "It was the *way* you said it. You were flirting shamelessly with me."

He pretended to be dumbfounded. "Gee, I thought flirting consisted of things like, 'I'd really looove to have dinner with you sometime—at my apartment.'"

"That isn't flirting. That I would call a veiled proposition."

He laughed. "'A veiled proposition.' That's good, I like that. So then, what exactly *is* flirting, *Miz* Santisia?"

"I can't believe you'd ask me such a thing," she said, "when you seem so adept at it, Mr. Brothers."

He'd felt her hand grow warm on his since the letter *A*, and now it was warmer still. He realized with a kind of tortured glee that she, too, played the game, however idly.

"Well, since this is obviously going to take a long time, getting through the alphabet, why don't we take a break?"

"But you're only on *C*."

"I know, but you don't mind, do you? After all, you get paid by the hour."

She rolled her eyes, but smiled. "Okay, I have to go to the powder room anyway. I'll be back," she said and was out the door.

Jerome sank back against the cushions, adjusted his glasses, and sighed heavily. Outside, there were huge autumn tress nodding and bowing slowly in the breeze, and for a moment, a series of freeze-frame images flashed through his mind, images of Maria and him in the park, Maria and him over dinner by firelight, Maria and him driving along on backroads, singing along with a song on the radio, Maria and him in a passionate embrace, his cheek against her warm bare shoulder....

And then it hit him with terrible clarity: why would she? Would *he* be interested in someone with only one hand or arm, or foot, or leg? He would have liked to think it irrelevant, but realistically, it was unlikely.

No, she was only his therapist, his counselor, and before long, a few weeks at best, she would be gone, and he would be alone—perhaps forever, now that he was no longer whole. He slumped deeper into the cushions and wondered whether he could accept this, whether he even ought to. She came back at that moment, brisk and cool, as if nothing had happened, no spark had been lit, which, he realized, might well be the case.

"Now, where were we?" she said as she came up to his side of the sofa. "Letter *D*?"

"Yeah, letter *D*." He reached for the pencil and glanced down at the clumsy *A, B, C* he had already written.

She put her hand back on his to guide it, and it was cool now, almost cold, as if she'd washed in ice water. He shuddered inwardly.

"Okay," she said, "nice and easy," and they continued through the alphabet in silence.

She was too pretty, he decided, that's what it was. She was pretty in a sisterly sort of way, as if meant to be regarded only with mild admiration. And yet the emotion was not platonic: part of him wanted the certainty that a woman that good looking couldn't possibly possess depth of character, but another longed for her like she was the cure to some terrible illness.

He realized, crushingly, the tyranny of infatuation. It leveled him like a weight, and that angered him, conveniently drawing his focus away from his true anger, the way slamming his thumb in a car door would have "relieved" a toothache. It was simple infatuation, pitiless and irrevocable as the sunrise.

Damn it, he thought, she could at least have some glaring defect. She did not.

And now the convenient wall, the barrier he had previously tossed up around his heart with casual effortlessness, was gone. He sat before her like a child, defenseless, naked, hurting. It was scary, and glorious, and maddening, and it hurt. He could not help hoping that she misinterpreted it as frustration at the effort of writing left-handed, or she would surely read it in his eyes.

CHAPTER THIRTEEN

TURNING THE CAMARO into his friend Steve's driveway, the sudden reappearance of sun, which had been blocked momentarily by a giant tree in Steve's front yard, nearly blinded Johnny Caruso. The light stabbed his eyes, already glazed from the combination of a hangover and too much speed. "Shit," he said aloud.

He buttoned his denim jacket, flipped his long hair over the collar, and got out, rubbing his knuckles with his palm. He rapped on Steve's front door and waited.

Steve threw the door open with a flourish, like something he'd seen in a slasher movie, an absurdly exaggerated grimace accompanying the action. "Hey, dude! Come on in. Boy, you look like shit. Have a brew," tossing a can of Budweiser. "What's the real deal?"

Johnny popped the beer open and gulped three times, burping noisily. "Aah. I don't know, man. Fucking *beat*. Is Sandy comin' over?" The leather-jacket brunette from Johnny's party, and Steve's sometimes-girlfriend, Sandy was usually able to produce something to smoke.

"Yeah. She's bringin' over Dweeper and Ronnie Mazursky. They're bringin' a bag a' sense." He brushed a lock of brown hair back.

"Aw, no way! Sinsemilla?" He drew himself up, putting on a swagger and a cowboy drawl: "Gen-you-wahn sayen-suh-meel-ya? Where the hell did they scare that up from?"

"I dunno. Some guy in Johnson City, Ed or Fred or something. Supposed to be *killer*."

Johnny swigged his beer. "Cool beans, man. I could use a bong hit or three—take the edge off." He plopped on a chair amid littered clothes and magazines.

"Yeah, a hit or three," Steve laughed. "Or ten. Or twenty."

Johnny shrugged. "Well, y'know. Whatever it takes to get high—HAA!" He began to sing, "Get high, high, high, high, high... get hiiiiiiigh." He stopped. "Hey, you ever read Nietzsche?"

"Who?"

"Nietzsche. This German philosopher that Morrison read a lot of."

"I don't know, sounds pretty shady to me." His eyes searched the window. "Ah, here they are."

"All right!" Johnny jumped up, gesturing with a fist. "Time to get mighty well done."

"Yupyupyup. Come in, friends," swinging the door open again. "Plenty of room for everybody. Music's on the disc player, beer's in the fridge, and hey, make yourselves homely while I run up and get *the bong*," and with that he dashed up the stairs.

"Hey," said the leather-jacket brunette, Dweeper and Ronnie close behind.

"What's up," said Johnny. The three exchanged brief handshakes, everyone obviously more concerned with Steve's reappearance than conversation. Eventually, they all sat down, looking sullen and abashed.

"So what's up?" Dweeper rummaged in his pocket for a cigarette.

Johnny yawned. "Not much. Jus' hangin' out."

"This your place?" Ronnie asked.

"Nah. Steve's parents. They're up in Vermont, I think."

"Oh." There was a long silence.

Thankfully, Steve reappeared, bong in hand. "Okay, guys. Lemme just put some water in this bad boy and we'll be all set."

"Use ice, it's much better that way."

Steve assumed a British accent. "Right-o, old chap. Ice is best, 'e's right —" then, changing to his normal voice "— that should be your nickname, Caruso: the *Ice Man.*"

Johnny chortled as Steve disappeared again.

"Hey, Johnny," said Sandy, "did you hear anything about Jerome Brothers?"

Johnny coughed, annoyed. "Yeah, *he's* all right. My ol' lady went to visit 'im a couple times. He should be out inna few days, why?"

Her eyes widened. "Just curious." Her voice had a strange sing-song tone, like *I-know-something-you-don't-know,* much icier than at the party. No one else seemed to notice.

"Yeah," said Ronnie, "I heard about that. That was a weird accident: guy fell out a tree in your yard and got his arm run over by the friggin' train, huh?"

"His hand. Just his hand."

"Whatever, man. Boy, how old is that guy, anyway?"

Johnny shrugged. "I dunno twenty-seven, twenty-eight?"

"You got some old friends, dude. Boy, that musta been something. He musta rolled all the way down that hill like a fuckin' beachball, huh?" He laughed, a snorting, brutal laugh.

Sandy slapped his leg. "Ron! It's not funny. I was *there.*"

"I'm sorry," he said, mock-sheepish. "But boy, he musta gone down that hill like a sack of potatoes!"

They all laughed except the girl, who stood up, indignant. "If you guys don't cut the shit, I'm gonna leave. I mean it."

Steve returned from the kitchen. "What's this?" he said. "You're gonna leave? Hey, that's cool, more for us!"

The three burst into cackles.

"That's it," she said, heading for the door.

"Hey, I was just kiddin'," Steve said, following. He turned to the others. "Man, what's with her? I was just kiddin' around," he called. "Did I miss something here?"

Johnny shook his head, unsmiling. "Women. Can't live with 'em, can't shoot 'em. Pass the bong, bro."

And with that, Steve was silenced.

PART
TWO

CHAPTER FOURTEEN

CHESTNUT AVENUE WAS the main route, the only main route, through Carverville. Like a living cliché of small-town America, it contained the usual quaint gas station, a post office of sorts— recently renovated with smaller boxes and computers, along with a sandstone courthouse, and general store: Macy's Market, on the corner of Chestnut and Hawthorne. Macy had been dead since long before the Civil War, but the shop, owned and operated by Tom and Phyllis Atkins, whose ten-year-old son David had leukemia, still retained the flavor of an era nearly forgotten.

Great smoked sausages hung from the walls, right alongside rakes and straw brooms, huge barrels of sawdust squatted in front of the wooden counter, and the soda and juice section boasted jars of homemade pickles and relishes. In addition, the Atkinses sold cigarettes and toilet paper, magazines, ice cream and hot pretzels and hot dogs, canned goods and dog food, a soup of the day, and hero sandwiches. The diverse and regular clientele, mostly locals like Jerome who were on a first name basis with Tom, if not Phyllis and Tom, always got a friendly "Mornin'!" with their coffee or a "How's Billy's leg comin' along?" with their bread and eggs.

Occasionally a stranger wandered in, someone from out of town asking for directions or just stopping to stock up on cigarettes. The inevitable fatuous exclamations followed: "Oh my God, this is soooo cute! Dan, look at this place it's like something out of Norman Rockwell can you believe it?" And behind his bifocals, smiling knowingly to himself, Tom thought "Mm-hm" and said, "You folks have a nice trip now, hear?" Tourists.

Today Tom sat all alone in the store. It was a fine time to be alone there, mid-morning, with sunlight streaming in on the rows of cans and boxes, making a little glare on the countertop. He felt a mellow stirring in his heart, a strange awareness of something deep and abiding and full of fruition that seemed a part of the time of year, inexorably bound up with the play of sunlight along the countertop, the near cloudless sky and huge trees standing resplendent in autumn colors. Yet that was not all: a sense of loss, a feeling that this intimation of the pure white joy at the heart of things was merely transient, a presumptuous bit of earthbound arrogance: a stained-glass shadow.

Of course, that doubt was connected somehow with the seeming injustice of things—Jerome Brothers' tragic accident, which had shocked and saddened both him and Phyllis, and of course, Davy, his poor ten-year-old body racked with pain, trying to hide it though it shone like summer from his brown eyes. Leucocytosis, leucocythemia, leucocythaemia: leukemia. Too many colorless corpuscles. And how he longed to fix it, to give the boy *his* blood, all of it, whatever it took: take the pancreas and liver, too, yes, take the goddamn heart and marrow and brain and kidneys and everything, just live, damn it. Just live.

Ah, well. C'est la vie, right? Nothing was to be done now except to wait: trust the doctors, but bargain with God. O Holy Father, take my wife from me if you must, take me and tie me to an anthill in the desert sun, lash me with thorns and nettles, tear me to pieces, shred me slowly, but please please God please let him live.

But it was no use after all. A selfish prayer, not a real one. "Thy kingdom come, thy will be done." But then there were the whys. Why, Lord? "Man was born to suffer as the sparks fly upward." He remembered:

We grope for the wall like the blind,
we grope like those who have no eyes;
we stumble at noon as in the twilight,
among those in full vigor
we are like dead men.
We growl like bears, we moan
and moan like doves;
we look for justice, but there is none;
for salvation, but it is far from us.

Phyllis came in, shattering the moment. Fortunately. "Morning, hon."

He smiled faintly. "Morning."

"Any of the breads come in yet?"

"Nope."

She came around to his side of the counter: a little woman, greying a bit but still attractive. "And how are you this fine October morning?"

"Okay," he said.

"Thinking about David?"

He sighed. "Yeah." A pause. "You know, that whole business with the Brothers boy…." He ran his hand through his hair.

"Terrible."

"Well, that's the kind of thing that sets me to thinkin'. It just don't seem *fair*. I mean, you work hard, you do what you're supposed to do, and…."

"And sometimes you get thrown a curve ball," she said gently. "I know. Believe me, I know."

He sat down, frowning, and his eyes filled. "It just don't seem fair."

"Well. You're right, it don't. But y'know, Tom, we just have to accept it. What was it you said the other day? 'Trust the doctors, but —'"

"'Bargain with God,'" they said together.

"Well, hell," he said.

"Well, hell."

CHAPTER FIFTEEN

MARGARET ROBBINS TOOK a long time to decide to leave her husband. Perhaps the decision was the inevitable outcome of a process, she thought, one that began the minute Ed was laid off, or even before. It might even have started at the beginning of their courtship.

Perhaps a snap decision, or one cemented in her sleep and confirmed in her waking hours: it was difficult to say. All she knew was that, one day, she would do it. She did not know when or under what circumstances or even whether she would break it in a certain way, or if perhaps she would just leave. But she knew that all the idle apartment-seeking in the classifieds, the long rides to work and back, the nagging thoughts and restive nights, all of it culminated in a clean break, in the weight of centuries lifting off her. But divorce. Such an ugly word, a scandal-maker. And on what grounds? Practically unheard-of in Carverville, divorce was like some taboo out of the 1920s. Like a two-piece bathing suit, she thought. Or a venereal disease. Normal people didn't get divorced; movie people got divorced, big city people got divorced.

Well, screw 'em all, she thought with renewed resolution. Perhaps she could enlist the support of Bill McCullough. He'd been through a "groundbreaking" divorce himself back in '89 which caused quite a stir. She sighed. Perhaps not. Either way, she would win, she would break free, pull the rug out from beneath this shoddy marriage, this mock romance. It was over, plain and simple.

On the day she finally decided to do it, she had been late for work, forgotten her lunch and had to resort to buying some pasty facsimile of a sandwich from the vending machine, had a horrifically busy afternoon, and received a ticket for failure to stop completely at a stop sign. After all that, the realization—after dinner, sitting back on the couch with the obituaries—should have been the proverbial last straw. But it was an epiphany, a moment of revelation and relief, as if light had just been let into her life.

Slowly she closed the newspaper, slowly rose, stretching her long arms above her, yawning. Patting her brown hair absently, she smiled a little secret smile. She would have to get used to this before she put it into action.

Ed scowled at her from behind his Miller. "What are you grinning at?"

"Nothing. Why?"

"I dunno," he grumbled. "Just funny that you're smilin' at the news when there's nothin' funny on."

It was true. The story playing out before them involved a satanic cult and their anti-Semitic ravings. It looked almost too absurd to be serious, but it was real.

She shuddered and scowled back at Ed, deliberate. "You're right. I'm sorry. I guess my sense of humor just isn't what it used to be."

"Huh?"

CHAPTER SIXTEEN

ELAINE MCCULLOUGH WAS having her afternoon cocktail. Teaching junior high history all day took its inevitable toll, and in addition to being a little on the heavy side, fortyish, and a chain-smoker of Parliaments when she wasn't in class, Elaine told herself it was perfectly okay for her to come home each day and pour a glass of half milk and half Southern Comfort over two ice cubes. Then, invariably, she collapsed on the couch, propped her feet on the coffee table, sat back with a Parliament, and sighed. Daily.

She was tired. She had been tired for a long time, and yet there was always a bit of tension everywhere she went, something she carried like a birthmark or a distinctive limp. Most people would feel a slightly relaxed sensation when she whirled away, leaving her trail of restless energy behind her. Even now, as she sat peering down with small black insect eyes at the dusty ashtray she had filled with lipsticked cigarettes, it was there, charging the very air about her like a perfume.

Bill would come home, hours later it seemed, jaunty in his perennial Mets cap and jacket, solid as a good mattress, smoking one of those godawful perfectos. That was okay, but lately there was something wrong with him, and it wasn't just her imagination. It was nothing concrete, almost as if he walked around, smiling and happy, reliable, yet something in his eyes or behind his smile just wasn't quite right, as if it was a fake Bill: a clone, or an impostor wearing a "Bill" mask. She shook off the image with a frown. Her mind drifted back in time to when she and Bill had been courting, and they'd sat for hours in a restaurant called The Oyster Bar just outside the tiny strip that composed downtown Carverville, listening to the jukebox:

> *The ragged clown is standing by the carnival parade*
> *A final scene is played*
> *And then he leaves behind another faceless town....*

Such a sad song, and yet such happy times! A warm glow overcame them then: the place was always autumnal, even in summer. Something about the candles on the tables, and the way the fading sunlight beamed down through the blinds onto those smooth tablecloths, suggested nostalgia, whispered insistently that these were irrevocably the good old days. It was bittersweet, to be sure, yet always conscious of itself and of its definable and defining joy: in fact, it was almost as if those hours, even as they glided slowly by, were waving frantically from a back wall, crying, *Here we are: cherish us, cherish us.*

She wondered if Bill had ever been aware of this, or in fact, if it had been only her imagination, or nostalgia. Who could tell? She dragged long and slow on her cigarette, wondering, deciding at last she could not describe it to him, that it was not important, after all.

And then she thought again of what troubled her, that eerie remoteness in him lately. It hadn't been there, or at least she hadn't noticed it, the last time they'd played cards with Margaret and Ed. To her own surprise, she wondered if he was having an affair, then tried to dismiss the thought.

No. No, he couldn't. Well, of course he could. He *wouldn't.* Never. Besides, she would have noticed other things, changes in his behavior beyond the strangeness. Men became overly solicitous when they had an affair, either in an effort to assuage their guilt or to throw their wives off the scent—possibly both. She'd read about that.

It had to be something else: work? Not likely, though he might just be getting bored. Was it her? Dear Lord, was he bored *with her?* An intolerable thought.

She dragged long and slow on her cigarette again, hand trembling. The affair idea kept nagging at her, a widening pulse in the pit of her belly that expanded like a balloon, like when we learn that someone we love has unexpectedly died and are seized with outrage at words incomprehensible, preposterous. There was nothing funny in it, yet she felt a sudden impulse to laugh at it, against it, as if that would quell it.

She heard Bill's key in the door.

"Hi dear," he called.

"Hi," she said, gulping her drink, hoping to finish before he noticed. Bill thought her combination of milk and liquor grotesque.

"How's work?" she called.

"Naht bad." Good God, he thought. Get ahold of yourself. Should've driven around the block or something. The grieving feeling, the grip he felt around himself, was still strong, and he struggled to shake it. *Look daddy*, it said.

He puffed the cigar, chewing on the end.

"How are you?" he asked as he came into the living room.

"Okay," she lied, rising to kiss him. "Tired. School was a madhouse today."

They pecked each other on the lips. "Isn't it always?" He recoiled a little because of the Southern Comfort, and pretended not to show it.

"It was *bad* today," she said, emphasizing the word with one hand up. "I collected two knives and—are you ready for this?—a gun."

He winced, more on the inside than outside. "Good God." His reaction was more because of Joey than out of concern for her, he realized. Elaine hated guns; and so do I, he thought ruefully. He sat down.

"Don't worry," she was saying, "it was empty. I think it was more for 'protection' than anything else. Either that, or the kid's selling drugs, God knows."

"I hope he was expelled."

"He was."

"Well." It sounded final, as if he was too tired, or too numb, to say more. "At least it wasn't loaded," he added.

"Yes," she said. "There is that." And sighed.

He sighed too, and the room grew suddenly quiet in that long suspiration. Outside, a flock of sparrows burst from the lawn, the sound a cross between the rotating blade of a helicopter and a leaf skittering on its back across an empty street.

"Everything go okay for you today?"

"Pretty much," he said. It was a good day, except for the last half hour or so. God damn October.

"Good. I was afraid there was something wrong. You seem..." oh God here it comes "...like there's something bothering you lately. I was beginning to worry...." She faltered there, lamely, letting it trail off, kneading her hands together in her lap.

He picked up the cue, his voice—in the broad Susquehanna accent they had in common—falling into the cadence of her speech: "Worried? Abowt me?" He laughed, a false indulgence, then stood so that he faced the fireplace, his back to Elaine.

"I'm serious! I thought maybe you were coming down with something." This was untrue, but Bill didn't see the telltale signs— fidgeting, averting her eyes—of her unskilled lying. He continued to face the fireplace.

"No, I'm okay."

"You're naht having an affair or something, are you?" she laughed. Oh God.

He wheeled around. "Very funny!" It was a shocked expression, a look of sheer incredulity. That type of joking was not funny.

"Just teasing you," she said, thinking, I can't believe I said it. "I know you don't like Margaret that much."

"Ma-*har*garet!" he puffed. "Honey, have you been staying home to watch soap operas? What an idea. Margaret." He was still shaking his head in smiling disbelief, but his expression was of thinly veiled disgust.

"I'm sorry. I just wondered."

He stopped his shaking, looked at her curiously. "Wondered what?"

"What's wrong," she said quickly. She was serious now, her eyes averted, like a child who has been caught in a lie.

"Nothin's wrong." Get ahold of yourself.

"Are you sure?" She looked up, questioning more with her eyes than with her voice.

"Sure I'm sure," he said. "Nothing's wrong." He sat down across from her, began to flip through the newspaper. "What could be wrong?"

CHAPTER SEVENTEEN

JEROME LEFT THE hospital at the beginning of November. Maria Santisia had again recommended prosthetics, stressing the realistic nature of artificial hands these days—*You can't even tell. Honest*—but he would hear nothing of it.

For a long time, the stump remained terribly sensitive, as if the hand was still there, a ghost hand he could picture in his mind's eye, and if someone had said, "Move your right thumb," he could have sworn he would be doing just that. It was like having had Louise Caruso present him with a hand that had been rescued from the pile of frozen carrots and green beans.

Louise had originally wrapped the hand in a towel, then rewrapped it in paper towels, and Jerome would always remember the sinking feeling when he was told it could not be saved. The towels had nearly disintegrated, mushy and clotted with blood, ruining any chance of reconnecting vital nerve tissues and arteries. Afterward, the stump had been wrapped in bandages, the wound dressed, and the end formed into a rounded shape that conformed to the bandages.

It was an extremely frustrating transition altogether, particularly when it came time to get dressed, but Maria continued to be there for him every day. At his own request, he'd been discharged early as a "homecare" patient, and he paid her directly for her services, for the sake of simplicity and economy. She was allowed to work with him at home, continuing with occupational therapy, although her insistence upon doing so had made her begin to question her own motives. What was it about Jerome Brothers—he wasn't, after all, that good-looking—that made her want to keep seeing him, that made them perhaps a little more than friends?

She pondered this as she drove her old Ford along the overpass, heading toward Jerome's from nearby Waverly. She'd expected Carverville to be bigger, and its simplicity charmed her, making her wonder why she hadn't known the town existed. She'd also expected Jerome's place to be an apartment, and was surprised and impressed that he owned his own home, the sight of it making the recollection of his relative poverty slip from her mind, it being a house, after all: unpretentious, but a house all the same.

She rounded the corner and headed up Dixon Street, toward her first glimpse of the old house. One, two, three...there it was, the fourth one on the left. She swung into the driveway, smiling to herself as she saw his face beside the drawn-back curtain. That moment would be forever etched into her memory, the house, the face beside the curtain glimpsed momentarily before the curtain swung back into place, it drove a warm turbulence up from the depths of her spirit, suffusing her face with its hot urgency. She shook her head. Across the street a dog barked, and the sound made her feel how completely over summer was. The sky was emptied of stars, a cold breeze made her shudder as she reached back to knock on the door.

Grinning, Jerome opened it before she could knock. "Hi there."

"Hello," she said. "May I come in?"

An odd, constrained look darkened his eyes. "Why not?" he said. "I'm in a good mood."

She entered primly, letting him hold the door open for her. "You're in a good mood," she said. "That's great." She sounded unconvinced, she knew, as if she actually believed he ought to be in some other sort of mood. She gave her head a tight shake. Why so self-conscious?

"Would you like something to drink?" He led her into the kitchen, more with his eyes than with any gesture.

"Maybe some water."

He grinned impishly. "Just water? Or do you want ice?"

"Yes," she sighed, sinking into a chair—poising herself on it, actually— "with ice, please." His ironic tone exasperated her. She had ceased to be a child a long time ago, and it irked her that he should be so unconstrained. And so silly.

He arched an eyebrow. "Something wrong?"

"No," she said, and suddenly meant it. "I'm just a little tired."

"Tough day at the office, eh, honey?" he said in a ridiculous falsetto that made her laugh out loud. God, he was irreverent.

"No," she said when she'd stopped laughing. "I don't get an office. My 'office' is any one of a thousand rooms."

"Ooh, I like that," he said, still falsetto. "You sound like a traveling salesman."

"Sales*woman*."

"Sales*person. Miz* Santisia..."

She shook her head. "You're nuts." He answered with only the most placid and harmless of smiles, and she looked at him a bit guardedly. It's sweet, she thought of that smile. Too sweet. There's a vampire in there. "So, are we ready for our lesson?"

"Is that the imperial 'we,' or are you talking to *me* about *my* lesson?"

Why was he being such a smartass? He was still grinning, and the cutting tone behind the grin baffled her. "Yes," she said patiently.

"That was an either/or question, Miz Santisia. Oh, I'm sorry: may I call you 'Maria?'" The grin faded to mock-serious.

He's hot, he's really hot, she thought. "No," she said, shaking off the thought. "I mean yes. *You* know that: Maria, Marie, Mare, Rea—well, no, not 'Rea.'"

He was looking gravely at her, his eyes velvety beneath the long lashes. "Why are you looking at me that way?"

"What way?"

"Like I'm —" she groped "— like I'm *fascinating*."

"I'd look at you that way if I were a three-headed iguana." She laughed, not sure whether to be offended or pleased.

Blood mounted to his cheeks, as if he knew he stood on dangerous ground. "I'd look at you that way if *you* were a three-headed iguana." He curled his fingertips as if holding a cigar and waved his hand around near his face, leering like Groucho Marx while she laughed.

"There's no such thing as a three-headed iguana," she said, maternally serious.

He arched the eyebrow again, scowling.

"Is there?"

He burst out laughing.

"I knew there wasn't!" she said, but he was laughing so hard now it looked like it was hurting him.

"Oh, God, oh," he laughed, subsiding at last into panting, and looking dazed when he was able to stop. "Oh, man, that was too funny."

"I don't know about you," she shook her head at him, but she did know about him, or at any rate, she felt she did. Petulance overtook her, a longing both to push him away and to clasp him in her arms.

But it all felt wrong in that they were not supposed to end up together. They were supposed to become friends, maybe, for a little while, but nothing more. As he had predicted, she was supposed to spend a few weeks working with him, then walk away forever—driving down the road out of Carverville, far away from this cunning, enveloping warmth that threatened to bury her alive.

"You don't *want* to know about *me*," he said. "Remember, I was a poli-sci major in college. Poli-sci majors are notorious for going on incredibly long tangents about Greek and Roman civilizations...."

"Oh, really, now."

"I'm serious," he said, and he was off and running again, like it was a well-rehearsed routine. "And not only that," he went on, "we have this really annoying tendency to try to take all our knowledge and place it within a historical context —"

"Mm-hm..."

"— and then try to explain what's happening to, oh, twenty-first century man, for example."

"Within a historical context, of course." She smiled.

"Oh, of *course*." He returned the smile.

"Can we start your handwriting practice while we're discussing this?"

"Sure."

She drew out some paper from a large bag with cloth straps. "Okay," she said, and they began. "So what's it all about, Mr. Historical Context? What's happening to twenty-first century man—and women?"

He began to write before he replied. "Well," he said. "What's happening to twenty-first century people is this thing called automation. We're talking about a world run by machines: mechanization, computerization. The souls of men and women being drained away by these machines that bleep and blip and whirl around inside with all sorts of crazy goddamn electrical currents and then spew out 'data.' We're talking about the end of the human *race*," he said, breathing the word out as he bore down hard on the letter *B*.

She grimaced. "Look, I'm a medical person. I use machines every day. Don't you think you're exaggerating a little? I mean, isn't technology more good than bad?"

"No," he said. "It's so insidious, we're not even aware of it." He made a *C*. "Look at something like the Internet. There are actually people out there now who are more interested in looking at a computer monitor all night than they are in spending time with their own kids. And do you have any idea how many TV commercials the average American sees in a single year? Let me just ask you this: how much of what you see in the media do you think is true?" He realized with embarrassment that he was speed-talking.

"I don't know—most of it, I would think."

"Exactly. And why not? But you're only getting half the story, if that. You know why?" He did not wait for an answer. "Because the news programs and public affairs programs are almost all controlled by people who are connected with either big business or the government itself. And hardly anyone even questions it, except maybe on college radio or the editorial pages of some newspapers. So there's inevitably some twisted perspective involved, or the bland assumption that a mass of well-selected facts adds up to 'reality.' *It doesn't.* From even the most limited historical perspective, you can see —"

"Jerome," she groaned, "I'm not kidding now, come on. Not everyone cares about history, or media, or computers. It's hard enough to get by without worrying about all this stuff —"

"The whole problem is right there! It's such a challenge to get along today that very few people can afford to give a damn, to take the time to read Noam Chomsky or...or whoever. Net result: people struggling just to maintain the status quo, if possible. And they let themselves be brainwashed by plastic robots trying to sell them video games and—and—string cheese."

"String cheese?"

They both laughed. "Well, you know what I mean. Everyone got very concerned, it seemed, with everyone else, back in the sixties: then along comes the 'me' generation, and all kinds of people start turning into yuppies and money-grubbers. By the time the eighties ended, people had not only stopped fighting back, a lot of them had stopped caring about the fight. Women began getting co-opted again, racism just got subtler, but more insidious...and people just let things slide. History will probably repeat itself, since things are in such obvious turmoil now, and no doubt history will also judge this last generation very harshly, not only for their apathy and materialism, but for plain shortsightedness. They won't be vindicated. I mean, just look at environmental issues: it's no longer some trendy fad for Hollywood and Madison Avenue to cash in on. It's life or death."

"But Madison Avenue will cash in on it, more and more, and what gets done will only be the result of some big business' projected profit margin, or tax write-off, or whatever. What gets done will be like putting a bandage on a major chest wound."

"Exactly," he said. "You got it." His eyes gleamed like the eyes of a cat in the dark.

She looked at him coolly. "Can we continue with the practice?"

"Oh. Sorry." He picked up the pencil again.

"Actually, you're doing pretty well on your own. Why don't you continue through the alphabet, and I'll just watch?"

"Okay." He leaned forward, about to resume. And then suddenly, they were face-to-face, his eyes big and full of meaning. She had leaned forward too, unintentionally, and it seemed impossible that they had gotten this close.

"Mr. Brothers," she whispered.

"Miz Santisia," he breathed back softly. He reached a tremulous hand to her cheek, and their lips met, fully and with finality. Each felt an instant of hesitation from the other, and then there was only a softness and sweetness, a sadness, a fullness, and the brightest of lights. Something in her sang with fear, love, wonder.

When the moment ended, the kiss fading, they looked at each other again, searchingly. Her eyes were huge, searching and pained, like a cornered animal's.

"What's wrong?"

She smiled, and the pained look receded. "Nothing," she said. "Only—hold me," and she buried her face in his shoulder.

He clasped her to him, his right arm behind her clumsily, as if it were aware of its own clumsy handlessness.

They kissed again, passionately, and desire rose within her.

"Are you okay?" he said.

Her fingertips lifted to his temple and brushed back soft hair, and she felt his pulse beneath beating like some fluttery bird. "Yes," she said, "only...."

He waited. "Someone else?"

She heaved a sigh, sat back and smoothed her skirt. His eyes snapped shut a moment, as if he resented her ending the moment with this prim movement.

"It was a long time ago," she said. "He was married."

He said nothing, only nodded.

"He was an *arrogant* fuck." The curse snapped through the room. "Tried to 'buy' me with money and jewelry. It didn't work." She sighed again and touched her hand to his forehead. "Sonofabitch."

"I'm sorry."

"It's okay. I'm the one who should be apologizing. I wouldn't have brought it up, but—memories." She waved a dismissive hand in the air. "I'm sorry, I just had to get that out. I've been... alone for a while now. Self-supporting. I didn't expect —" she waved again, encompassing them, the room, all of it "— this."

"Me neither." He smiled and pulled her close, gently, and she yielded.

And then they were together, truly together above the forgotten pen and paper, the banal discipline of therapy. Everything had changed, as if everything had begun and ended, and begun again. He led her toward the couch, rapturous, in a kind of haze. He kissed her there, and just for a moment, she stopped him again, although she did not pull away this time. His mouth tasted faintly of peppermint.

"Jerome..."

"Ssshhhh."

"I —"

He touched a finger to her lips. "Please." It was a whisper, scarcely audible. "I just want to be with you," he said simply.

She understood. And, more, she felt the same. She clasped him with renewed passion, kissing him with the soft fervor of infatuation and innocent desire, her fingers fluttering at the buttons of his shirt. He held his hand against the back of her head lightly, as if handling something infinitely fragile, his fingers entangling themselves in her curls.

And then she was drawing him down to the couch, awkward and insanely hot among the soft crush of pillows, and she could feel his heart beating faster as she pressed herself against his breast. It was too good to last, she felt, but she surrendered with utter abandon, swirling his tongue around hers in a kiss that was deep and soulful. They parted for an instant, and before he could speak she moved slowly down his body, planting kisses on his chest, his stomach, unbuttoning as she went. She pulled his shirt out so that it hung loose about him, and he groaned as she kissed his chest, rising back to kiss his lips again and raking her fingernails lightly across the back of his neck.

"Wait a minute," she said.

He waited. Finally, he said, "Ye-e-es?"

She looked at him. "Are we going to do what I think we're going to do?"

"That depends. What do you think we're going to do?"

"You know," she said in a girlish whisper: "Sleep together."

"Oh," he said. "Well. Do you want to?"

"Do you?"

He smiled. "Don't answer a question with a question."

"*Do* you?"

The smile faded. "God, yes," he said.

"Good." She smiled and they came together again tenderly, kissing like lovers, with familiarity and comfort, then passionately, almost frantically, and his hand, hot and urgent, explored the small of her back with a tantalizing delicacy.

She stood, silently looking into his eyes, and led him toward the bedroom door. She seemed to know where she was going. He let her lead him, only looking at her. She led him into the bedroom. Silently, he followed.

And without a word, she undressed him.

When she had removed everything but his underwear, she realized what had happened, or rather, what was not going to happen. She paused.

"Jerome," she said finally.

"Yes?"

"What's wrong?" she said.

"I'm afraid you've, uh, taken me to the point of no return." He glanced down significantly.

"You mean —" She understood all in an instant. "I'm sorry, Jerome," she said.

"It's all right…."

"Are you okay?" She put her hand gently on his shoulder. "Does it hurt?"

"No, no," he said, but not convincingly. "I'm afraid we've spent just a *bit* too much time engaged in, ah —"

"Foreplay?" She laughed, a rich and throaty laugh that nearly made up for everything.

"You really had me going," he said, shaking his head and smiling.

"I did, didn't I?"

"Well," he said. "Yeah. Hey, listen, I'm sorry that —"

"Ssh." She touched a finger to his lips. "Don't say a word. Besides," she said, standing, "I don't usually do this sort of thing on the first date anyway."

He looked gravely at her. "You call this a date?"

Bursting into laughter together—great peals of laughter that shook them both—they embraced again, laughing still as they collapsed in a heap on the floor.

CHAPTER EIGHTEEN

LOUISE CARUSO OFTEN found herself transported back to that time when she was twelve and a bottle of pop was ten cents. Today, she was floating along placidly in one of these memories, letting her fingers get waterlogged as she scrubbed another pan, when the slam of the back door broke her reverie. For a moment, fear leaped and froze within her: Johnny was home.

"What's happening, Louise?" he shot as he strode into the kitchen. "Tough day at the office, or what?"

She turned a slow, long-suffering look on him, noticing his red eyes and dishevelled hair. "I do wish you wouldn't call me that. I can remember when you called me *mommy*."

He snorted. "No fooling. Hah." Air from his lungs drifted past, smelling of whiskey.

It's just a phase, she thought vainly. Just a phase. "How was school? Did you —"

"FUCK school," he barked.

She looked helplessly at him. "I *do* wish you wouldn't use that language in this —"

"Right," he interrupted. "So, what's for dinner tonight, Louise? Hog jowls and chitlins? Maybe some paaah-sum? Huh?"

"Johnny, please...."

"'Johnny, please,'" he mimicked. "What a joke."

Louise returned to the pan, watching as the water bounced from it, prismatic in the setting sun.

"So come on. What's it gonna be? Surf n' turf? Sheesh kabob? Nookie nookie?"

"Please go to your room," she said.

"WHY?" he shouted. It echoed once in his mind, a plaintive note: why?

"I just need to get these things done, and then —"

"What for?" he snapped, and now he felt the rage bubbling up inside him, swelling up into his throat. "Dontcha wanna *talk*? HUH? You wanted to know what a swell fuckin' day I had in school, didn't ya? Huh? Let's talk!"

He pulled up a chair, bouncing it against the floor deliberately, and slammed himself into it. It felt good, brutal and pure, to make himself stationary while the anger boiled up. Beads of sweat appeared on his forehead. "So. Let's talk." He dropped his voice to a sharp whisper. "Talk."

She braced herself. "Not when you've been drinking."

"Drinking?" He jumped back up, hair waving wildly. "What the hell does that have to do with it? Huh? A little nip and tuck with the guys after school? Hey, I had a *long day*, Louise. I had two tests today. How d'ya s'pose I *did*, eh? Drinking." He spat on the floor, a dark globule of phlegm.

"That DOES it!" she cried. "I don't care if you had ten tests today, you little shit! Clean that up, NOW!" She had slammed the pan down into the water and pointed at the floor with a trembling finger. Tears jumped to her eyes.

"Little shit?" He grinned. "Little shit?"

"I said clean it up. Now." She was livid, on the verge of hysteria.

"Little shit. How about that, she knows a baaad —"

"NOW!" she shrieked.

He glared at her, wavering. "Clean it up yourself," he said, and slouched out of the room, smiling bitterly.

"Johnny!" she shouted after him, but he was down the hallway already, hands in pockets, whistling drunkenly.

"Johnny," he said beneath his breath. His falsetto imitation of her was near-perfect. "John-ny."

She grabbed the pan, storming after him, her face set like a bronzed chicken. Wisps of her iron-grey hair seemed to float above her face as she clicked down the hall. "Johnny."

He halted. "Whatcha gonna do, Louise?" he drawled. "Ya gonna hit me with that fryin' pan?" He smiled viciously.

"Now you just shut up and listen to me —"

"What?" His eyes blazed. "*What?*"

"I said shut up and —"

He seized her arm and she dropped the pan, paralyzed, his grip like some steely claw digging into her soft flesh.

"Nobody, Louise—nobody—tells me to shut up. Okay?" His teeth clenched, sweat trickled down his forehead.

"Let go of my arm, you bastard."

"Did you hear what I said?"

"Let go, you —" She tried to hit him.

"Nobody!" he screamed, flinging her back. He pointed a finger in her face, glaring as if she were a demon. "*Nobody* fucking tells me to shut up."

For a moment an image of himself flitted through his memory: he was in his room, curled into a corner, hugging his knees. Tears ran slowly down his face, and he was cursing softly. He shook the thought off angrily.

"I'm leaving. You can get your own goddamn dinner." She burst into tears and turned quickly down the hall. She was in the living room seconds later, her body racked with sobbing.

"Fine!" he yelled. "Have a nice day!" He flung the pan down the hall and it bashed against the doorframe, leaving a broad dent before it clattered to the floor. Storming into his room, he slammed the door so hard that the frame itself shook, then turned the radio on with a savage shove of his finger, almost knocking the stereo to the floor. He turned the music up as loud as it would go.

CHAPTER NINETEEN

THEY WERE DRIVING down route seventeen into Johnson City, the sun beating down feebly on what was left of the leaves, and Jerome caught the almost-white glare of it from a newspaper box which bore the legend "Au Courant." He smiled humbly at Maria, giving her a slow sidelong glance. She caught the glance and returned the smile warmly. They had been together all day, and it was glorious. The phrase *too good to last* rang in his head like the sound of someone pinging a crystal glass with a fingernail.

He felt good, contented but slightly fatigued, and he yawned behind his hand. They'd spent a late night together the previous evening, and he rose early that morning to look for work. The mortgage company had replaced him while he was in the hospital—they were sorry, they'd said, but they needed someone full time. And so he was tired, but content, sluggish in a restful way, like on most Sundays.

She broke the silence suddenly: "Do you ever pray?"

It was an unexpected question. "No. Do you?" He looked almost incredulous, as if awaiting a punchline.

"Sure. Every day."

"Really?"

She smiled. "Uh huh. Did you ever pray? Like when you were a kid?"

"Well, no. My parents were killed in a car crash —"

She winced. "Oh, I'm so sorry."

"It's okay. Anyway, I was raised by my aunt and uncle, and they weren't very religious. I think we're Methodists...?"

"So you never had to pray."

"No. Well, I did pray once." He forced a laugh. "It was pretty recent: when I was in the hospital, actually, after my accident. I, uh—asked for help, I guess you could say."

"Help?"

"To deal with—you know," he fumbled. "To *cope* —?"

"With the accident."

"Yeah. Exactly."

"And did it work?"

"No, I don't think so," he mused. Then, firmly: "No."

"Well, why don't you try it again?" She said it gently, quietly, less a suggestion than a statement.

He shifted, scowling a little. "If I learned one thing in college, it was to avoid three topics of conversation."

"What are they?" she smiled.

"Religion is one...."

"But I'm not *talk*ing about religion."

He smiled. "Aren't you gonna ask me what the other two are?"

"What's the second?" she asked, rolling her eyes.

"Politics...."

"And....?"

"And the Great Pumpkin."

She laughed, and shook her head. "You're really nuts, you know that?"

"Certifiable."

She smiled, and it occurred to him that her smile really did make him feel like someone had just turned the light on for him.

"But *any*way," she was saying, "I wasn't talking about religion. I was just —"

"I know, I know," he waved it away with his hand. "You were just gonna say that it doesn't mean you're a religious fanatic just because you pray. I understand *that*."

"That's not what I was going to say," she said coldly.

"I'm sorry. What were you going to say?" His voice had taken on an edge.

"I was going to say that just because you prayed and didn't get what you asked for doesn't mean you'll never get it. Prayer isn't necess—"

"Prayer is a way that people kid themselves into thinking that some white-haired grandfather-type Guy in the Sky is gonna take care of 'em."

She threw her hands in the air. "I don't know why I even bothered."

He glared at her. "What do you mean?"

"Just that," she snapped. "I never should have brought it up."

"Why? What the hell difference does it make?" His voice rose.

"Apparently none."

"Well, Jesus Christ, whaddya think's gonna happen? I'm gonna grow another *hand?*" He thrust the stump toward her, the gesture almost obscene.

"No, Jerome. But maybe you'd stop feeling so sorry for your-self, all right?"

"What!?"

"Yeah. Sorry for yourself."

"Hey, *listen, lady*, I've got a fucking good reason to feel sorry for myself —"

"Here we go...."

"Yeah, here we go. I lost my hand, okay? *It sucks.* I have to spend twice as much time doing everyday ordinary bullshit as nor-mal people do, and I don't exactly feel like getting down on my knees and thanking your precious God for any of it. All right?"

She exploded: "Can you *walk?* Can you *talk?* Not everyone can, you know..."

"Oh, gimme a break."

"Yeah, right, give *me* a break. You play the stoic pretty well, Mr. Brothers, but you're bullshitting yourself. And you know what? I've seen a lot of hurting people in my work, and believe it or not, a lot of them have been hurting a hell of a lot more than *you*."

He was silent, furiously immobile and trembling with rage.

"And some of them were born that way." She paused, on the verge of tears.

"Fine," he snapped. "Good for them."

"Shit," she said and pulled over.

"What the hell are you doing now?"

She burst into tears. "I can't drive like this," she sobbed, and buried her face in her hands.

He looked out the window, numb.

"God*damn*it." She slapped the dashboard with her hands, then cried unabashedly, great rasping sobs that rocked her whole body.

"I don't believe this," he said coldly.

"What!?" she said through her tears. "What don't you believe?"

"Forget it. I'm outta here." He opened the door.

"Where are you gonna go?" She regained some control, and some anger. "Are you going to *walk* to the mall?"

He leaned back in. "Yeah. Yeah, I am. I'll hitch a ride back, thanks."

"Fine!" she said, choking back another sob. "Good riddance."

"You can bill me for the writing lessons," he said. "And for your other services," and with that he strode away.

"SCREW YOU," she screamed after him, but he did not turn back. She slumped back in the seat, clutching the steering wheel. "You bastard. You bastard."

CHAPTER TWENTY

WHEN THE ROBBINSES and McCulloughs got together for a night of card-playing, whoever hosted found it impossible to do anything other than pull out all the stops. They cleaned house thoroughly—floors scrubbed, curtains washed, furniture vacuumed—and tonight, a neighbor babysat the McCulloughs' pets on account of Ed's allergies. Elaine and Bill were ready early, and they looked as well-groomed as if they'd planned to spend the evening at someone else's house.

"Honey?" Bill called as Elaine came out of the bedroom.

"Yes?" She was adjusting a skirt that looked too tight on her bulgy hips.

"Did you remember to get beer for Ed?"

"No," she called, leaning back against the doorjamb. "I forgaht, dear. I guess he'll have to settle for scotch."

Bill met her in the hallway. "I don't think we even have any," he said. "I think all we have is Stolie and maybe some schnapps."

"Do we have any orange juice?"

"Honey, you *know* Ed doesn't drink screwdrivers. It's not a *man's drink.*"

She rolled her eyes. "Oh brother."

"Well, you know how he is. Say, would you do me a favor tonight, hon?"

"What's that?"

"Please, don't ask him abowt work."

"I wasn't going to," she said, eyebrows raised.

He held up his hands, backing off. "Okay, okay. Just making sure."

"I don't think he's found anything yet, anyway. I dowt if he's even looking. I ran into Louise Caruso last week at the mall—Friday? Yeah, Friday. Anyway, she said he hadn't found anything yet, and I dowt if he did this week. At this rate, Margie'll have to get a second jahb." She sat down, shaking her head.

"Let's naht even think abowt it, okay...?"

She looked up at him. "It's kind of hard naht to."

"I know. We'll just have to come up with other things to talk abowt, that's all. Ask them questions abowt the house, that sort of thing."

"The house!?"

"You know what I mean...."

"The goddamn house is falling apart." She laughed hard, erupting into a spasm of coughing.

He smiled. "Right, forget the house. But you know what I'm saying. Work is off limits, and any discussion abowt how they're getting along is totally owt of the question."

"What do you mean?" It hadn't occurred to her, oddly enough, that the marriage might be going bad.

"Well, I mean, I seriously dowt if they're getting along all that great. There's gotta be stress on the marriage as a result of Ed naht working." Christ, he thought, there's stress on *our* marriage.

She sat for a moment quietly, as if lost in thought. From outside, the coloratura of a bird's song broke the silence.

"I suppose," she said finally. She sounded almost sad, as if they'd just decided to remortgage the house or move to the city. The doorbell rang.

"There they are." He turned to go out, then turned back, grinning. "Remember —"

"Go answer the door," she said. "I know, naht a word."

He chuckled and walked away with a little spring in his step. After all, here he was, doing relatively well, and here was his old buddy Ed, going into a downhill slide, and coming to his house to smoke his cigars and drink up his booze. Bill saw all of this in a flash, and was ashamed.

He opened the door. "Well, well, look at you two. You look like you're ready for the Prince's Ball."

It was almost true: Ed's hair was slicked back, uncharacteristically neat, and Margaret wore a bright fuschia lipstick. Both were dressed neatly; almost, Bill thought, distinguished.

"*Bill*," Margaret exclaimed. "Nice to *see* you!" She gave him a kiss on the cheek, which she had never done before. Elaine caught a glimpse of this as she emerged from the other room.

Ed straightened up. "Howdy, stranger." He shook Bill's hand, brisk and overzealous. "Good to see ya, buddy. Gaht any 'a them perfectos? Heh heh heh."

"Sure, sure," said Bill, smiling warmly. "Come in, let me take your coats."

"Hi-ii," chimed Elaine. She clicked across the room in heels that were far too small for her, dragging on a Parliament, stubby arms outstretched in welcome.

"There she is," the couple said in unison. "How are you, dear?"

Elaine gave them each a peck on the cheek.

"We're fine," said Margaret.

"Fine," said Ed.

"Can I get you something to drink?"

"Do you have any wine?" Margaret asked. "I'd love some white wine."

"Certainly," said Elaine. She turned to Ed. "Ed...?"

"Sure," he said quickly. "White wine sounds great."

Bill's eyes widened. "*Eddy*. You sure you wouldn't like something else? I mean, I think we've gaht some Stolie, and maybe —"

"No, no," Ed said. "Wine'll be just great."

"Well, okay," said Elaine. They moved as a group into the kitchen. "Bill, will you get the cards owt while I pour everyone's drinks?"

"You bet." He rummaged in a drawer, poking under old credit card receipts and pencils in search of a deck of cards. He found a pinochle deck, saying, "Aha!" before he noticed what it was (they were setback players), then *Oh brother* beneath his breath while he began to search anew. He was preoccupied with the place on his cheek where Margaret kissed him, the notion of Ed drinking white wine—a novelty of no small magnitude—and the growing heartburn from a dinner eaten too hastily. He poked and lifted and prodded things in the drawer, coming up with a useable deck only after Elaine twice asked him if he was sure they were in there.

Once they began playing, things returned to normal. Ed took a perfecto and lit the large, torpedo-shaped cigar, to the mutual consternation of the ladies. The chatter grew loud, Ed shuffled loudly, the cigar pointing upward from the corner of his mouth, and Bill wondered how raunchy that white wine must taste after puffing on a cigar. His mind wandered farther and farther away until, lost in the blank stare he fixed upon the hand Ed just dealt him, he was jolted by Elaine's voice: "Bill."

"Huh?" He shook himself out of it.

"Jesus, honey, come back to earth. Ed needs your help here, and if you don't watch owt, Margie and I are gonna kick your butts!"

The evening progressed in the typical fashion: the men defeated the women in one game after another, until they decided to switch partners, and it became a contest between the teams of Margaret and Bill versus Ed and Elaine. Elaine hated having Ed as a partner, although one would have thought him an asset after watching him and Bill against the two women. But she knew that Bill was the true card shark; Ed was the weakest player of the four.

It all seemed less relevant as the evening wore on and the game was neither dominated nor surrendered by anyone in particular. Elaine simply noticed that Ed was getting louder and sillier, and that Margaret dealt with it by paying attention to Bill. Her husband had a certain steadiness and sturdiness that Elaine cherished, and it looked like Margaret was somehow trying to draw strength from that, possibly just admiring it.

For the first time in a long while, Elaine felt a surge of jealousy, and her recent comment about Bill having an affair bounded back into her mind with brutal clarity. She tried to drive it from her thoughts, and masked the effort with forced exuberance, but the thought continued to badger her. Eventually, she lapsed into silence and watchfulness.

Only once in the course of the evening did this discomfort manifest visibly. Bill watched Elaine guardedly as she shuffled. He and Margaret were partners in the game at that juncture, yet this did not seem to occur to Elaine: she only noticed Bill watching her as she shuffled, then glancing between her and Margaret.

Finally, when the tension rose so high in her that she felt a hot, hollow ball of fury in her throat, without warning she snapped, "What?"

It was awkward for everyone, although in different ways, like the instant after a person has sneezed during a quiet passage in a symphony. No one knows whether to choke back their indignation or vent it outright, to stifle their laughter or chortle like a horse. No one moves.

"What?" said Bill innocently.

"What are you staring at me for?"

"I was just watching you shuffle," he said. He sounded innocent, and flabbergasted. His lip trembled slightly, like a boy's.

"Well, what are you looking at *her* for?"

"I —" he fumbled "— I wasn't aware I was doing *any*thing."

"Well, no cheating," she said half-jokingly. She realized the comic irony of the word immediately, and its effect must have been written on her face, she thought. But she lapsed back into thoughtful silence.

When she was not thinking—or, at least, not concentrating steadily on the game—Bill noticed that she put her left hand gently against her glass and slowly stroked it up and down with her thumb and forefinger. Slowly and mindlessly, she stroked the smooth clear glass, her fingernails nearly touching it, but not quite. It was mesmerizing to watch, as when someone silently drums their fingers on a tabletop. Margaret noticed it, too, but said nothing. There was nothing to say, though it was certainly a strange image to take home at the end of the night.

CHAPTER TWENTY-ONE

ON A SUNDAY afternoon in November, after Ed Robbins walked out of Macy's Market with a bagful of groceries in each arm, Phyllis Atkins turned to her husband and said, "So whaddya think?"

Tom looked up from the comics. "Abowt what?"

"Ed and Margie Robbins."

"What abowt 'em?"

"Well. Don't you think there's some prahblems there?"

He folded his paper, slowly, laboriously, as if trying not to get annoyed at an interruption from a well-meaning child. Then he put his great hands on his knees and pushed himself up in the chair to straighten himself. He took a deep breath and slowly let it all out again. "The truth?"

She nodded. "What do you think?"

He paused again, like he was afraid to be the bearer of bad news. "I think their marriage is in the shitter."

"*No,*" she said. "Honey, don't say that, that's like a jinx."

"Well...."

"Don't you think that's a little premature?"

Tom took another long breath, then sighed it out with a patient vehemence. "No, I don't think it's premature. I think it's been a long time coming. Let me tell you a little something abowt Ed that you probably haven't heard me mention before. You remember when he was abowt—oh, I dunno—seventeen, eighteen?"

"Mm-hm." She appeared to relax a bit.

"Well, you and me were probably thirty, thirty-one at the time. Old Bill Hotchkiss, 'member him?"

"Of course...."

"Bill and I threw a party one night, and for some reason, Ed was invited. I think there was abowt twenty-five or thirty of us, all at this big hall that we'd rented owt in Oswego —"

"Where was *I*?"

"It was a stag party, dear...."

"Ohh...."

"And you only dance with your clothes *on*, from what I recall."

She clucked her tongue at him and tried not to grin.

"Now don't interrupt the story." He smiled. "Anyway, like I say, there was abowt twenty or thirty of us, and somebody decided to have a 'shahts contest.' Now, that entailed a competition of who could drink the highest number of shahts of hard liquor in a row, and no getting sick nor going to the bathroom, neither. And owt of all those men, who do you suppose come in first place in the shahts contest?"

"You're serious."

"Serious as a heart attack. And naht only that, he said—and, o' course, he was mighty drunk, but still—he said he was ready for more when he had already won the contest by a long shaht—no pun intended."

"So, what you're telling me is that you think Ed's got a drinking problem."

"Honey, that boy was able to put 'em away like a champ when he was that young, he's naht likely to get any worse at it. Now I don't know nothin' for sure, but he don't look too good these days, you know?"

"No. No, I guess he doesn't." She nodded. "So, your philosophy on the Robbins marriage is that it's in trouble on account of Ed's drinking too much."

"Well, I can't say I know it. I mean, I'm not sayin' he's gaht a prahblem or nothin', but it don't look good, y'know? 'Course, maybe it's just a case of the old magic goin' owt of it, I don't know." He shook his head.

She thought about it. "I don't know either. But I'd bet dollars to donuts that if they're havin' prahblems, it's on account of his naht workin'. I talked to Louise the other day, and she said she doesn't even think he's looking."

"Louise? Caruso?"

"Mm-hm."

"Well, what in the hell would *she* know about what's goin' on with the Robbinses?" He sounded almost angry with the nosy Louise Caruso.

"Damned if I know."

They sat quietly for a moment. Already they were beginning to look like their parents had in their twilight years: wise, ruminative, capable of enduring disaster upon disaster.

"Well," said Tom.

"What?"

"So what's new with our friend Louise? Other than the fact that she's mindin' everybody's business but her own?"

A trace of a smile crossed her face. "I don't know, hon. Apparently naht much, or she wouldn't be talkin' abowt other people so much."

"That son of hers still raisin' holy hell?"

"Oh yeah. He's been causin' some sort of trouble all along, but she says he's just goin' through a phase." She rolled her eyes.

"Let's hope she's gaht the gumption to throw him the hell *owt* if he keeps it up after high school. I wadn't no jewel myself in school, but these kids today are loony when it comes to raisin' cain. I think it's drugs, myself."

He turned a rheumy eye to his wife, slowly and deliberately.

"And I wouldn't be surprised if that boy doesn't live to be twenty-five," he said.

"Be able to be alone. Lose not the advantage of solitude."
— SIR THOMAS BROWNE

CHAPTER TWENTY-TWO

IT WAS A BRIGHT November morning, the kind of day that, if not for the colors of the trees, and the distinctive smell of woodsmoke, might be mistaken for a morning in May. Three low white clouds stretched across a cool sky, a burst of laughter from the miraculous last birds of summer echoed sharply in the air. Jerome breathed deeply, on his way back from a morning stroll.

He had tried not to dwell too much on the scene with Maria. He'd felt a tugging at his heart, but then anger welled up furiously, obliterating all else for a day or two. Then the anger cooled down into resentment, and the realization that it was all over, that it had never in fact begun, and was never meant to be, crept in and established itself in the guise of callous unconcern. And in that way, believing his own lie, he had carried on.

It was difficult today, somehow. A little more time had passed, resentment seemingly ebbed away, and the situation was no longer an issue. But he had not seen her, and that made all the difference.

He'd struggled since the layoff, although that particular crisis at least took his mind off the problem with Maria. He'd had to engage in a full-time job search, finding nothing for which he was qualified, then getting more and more desperate as food money ran out, bills piled up on the bureau, and the thought of approaching winter actually frightened him.

Finally, resolved to take the first job that came along, he did just that, and wound up selling vacuum cleaners for a well-known national company. Though humiliating and humbling, the occasional sale and the promise of a weekly paycheck of some sort made it seem more bearable. Besides, he had to take what he could get in a recession.

Now it was Saturday, and he had planned a much-needed day off although, theoretically, he should have been working. It was good to be out walking, enjoying the unseasonably warm morning: especially since, he realized, it might be the last temperate day in Carverville for many months. As he often did these days, he thought about the lost hand. He was still grieving it. The thought slowed him down, and before long, he found himself ambling along like a window shopper in a strange city, looking thoughtlessly at whatever he passed.

The old house slipped into view. He remembered the way he felt when his aunt and uncle bequeathed it to him, a guilty gratitude beneath which lurked an impulse to literally jump for joy. It was a beautiful old house, a small colonial with latticework repainted many times, and a frumpy old maple tree in front. He cherished it now more than ever, because Maria had been to see him there. He looked down at the sand along the edges of the road, where mica chips glittered in the sun like lights on the surface of the sea.

And then he was climbing up the front steps, fumbling with his hand for the keys, opening the door. He went in quietly and breathed a long, slow breath to try to relax himself. The walk had heightened his pulse.

Opening the classifieds, he flopped down on the couch, crumpling the paper in the process. In a few moments, he had second thoughts. When he got back up to turn on the TV, the paper slid slowly to the floor with a small hissing sound.

On the screen, a balding man with an eerie tenor sang, "Do you need someone to love? Don't you need a man to love?"

The camera panned slowly back to reveal the man's hand as it gently and idly stroked the shoulder of a woman's body. The woman was apparently asleep, but as the camera retreated from the scene, Jerome saw that the body was a corpse. He shuddered as his eyes widened.

"Jesus," he said beneath his breath.

That was disturbing enough to put a note of gloom into an otherwise bearable day. He flicked the TV off, retreated to the kitchen for a sandwich, then decided to bring the classifieds from the living room. He stared blankly at the newspaper's neatly columned page as he undid the little twist-tie that sealed the bread. A laborious process with one hand, he wondered for a moment why he even bothered to close the bag so tightly in the first place. He threw the twist-tie away.

Then, reaching into the plastic bag—it sat upright on the counter, balancing only by virtue of gravity—he pulled out the cutting board, took out ham, Swiss cheese, and mayonnaise, laying each on the counter with the precision of a blind man. He opened each package neatly, pulling hard on the flaps to get the stickers to unstick themselves, then piled meat and cheese on one slice of bread. Gripping the mayonnaise jar in the crook of his elbow—it was a new jar, the most grueling element of the whole project—he bore down on it, twisting ferociously, his lower lip working, and sweat beading his brow until the small popping sound signalled victory.

He sat down heavily on a kitchen chair, drained. His stomach heaved a little as he realized that the job of making a sandwich made him hungrier than he had already been. He stood back up, put away ham, cheese, and mayo, then drew a knife from the drawer beside the sink. A sharp carving knife with a smoothly polished edge, the blade glittered a bit wickedly in the afternoon sun.

He shook the thought off quickly, before it sounded too reasonable. Nobody, he told himself, gets *that* depressed. He knew that that was untrue, of course, but the alternative was inadmissible. And yet he could not help admitting that he'd hit an emotional low.

Outside the window, a cloud obscured the sun, and for a moment, all was grey.

He sat back down again, abruptly. The hell with it, he thought, and decided to go out again, taking half of the sandwich with him. A hike through the woods sounded like a good idea. Putting the other half of the sandwich in the refrigerator, he set out, locking the door behind him.

It had cooled off considerably, which was strange when he recalled that it was not yet noon. But the sky was clouding up, and the wind picked up leaves and scattered them across lawns. He walked down the road, bearing left at the first stop sign, then left at the next.

Eventually he came to a cul-de-sac surrounded by a wooded area. Orange "No Trespassing" signs dotted the trees, but he knew it would be a simple matter to lose himself in those woods for several hours with virtually no danger of being discovered. This was one of the few outstanding benefits of Carverville, this potential for peace and solitude.

As he walked among the trees he felt the heaviness of their silence, and the small chirping of birds that broke the silence was both surprising and welcome. He thought of how heavily laden the woods had been with plants and wildflowers during the summer months, when he'd gone on nature walks with his uncle as a boy. There had been strange lavender mushrooms, tendril-like in the damp sod, and great oaks covered with bluish lichen. Dark green moss grew on the many-rooted ground in summer, and his uncle always spoke with a reverence that seemed incongruous with his toughness about the many flowers: goldthreads, white lady's slipper, and bittersweet nightshade. Farther out, in the thick of the woods, they'd found the oddly majestic Queen Anne's Lace, flat-topped clusters of white with a single dollop of color in the center; Black-eyed Susans, those daisy-like flowers he always gathered in quantity for his aunt; and the treasured find, Virginia Bluebells, their flowers cornflower blue, trumpet shaped, hanging demurely down from arched clusters at the tips of the stems. As a general rule, nothing had been too good for his aunt Laura, his "mom," but Virginia Bluebells were "too pretty to pick."

And in the marshy places, in wet meadows and along the ponds and bottomlands, among the invincible uprisings of skunk cabbage and ferns, grew cattail, alder and iris, pink lady's slipper, and water lilies. Some he had seen only in books—Indian plantain, False Dragonhead, Tall Ironweed—but he had an idea of what they looked like. He kept an eye out for these unfamiliar treasures, although it was too late in the year for most.

Finally, he made his way out of the woods and into a strange neighborhood. He'd been walking for an hour, and was no longer in Carverville, not at all thinking of the direction, not even caring. Now he walked along the unfamiliar road, breathing hard, a curious tune in his head like the loud harsh whispering of wind in the trees, the cracking of unfreezing branches in springtime.

Along the roadside lay shards of discarded plastic, a piece of square ribbed cardboard that, from a distance, looked like a package of graham crackers, and an empty bottle of Fleischmann's. It made him sad, somehow, to think of what people threw away, and how often they threw it these days. And that tiny passage of music rose and fell in his head, curiously soothing, a scrap of melody.

Then, a sudden disruption to his serenity, he thought of work, and the humiliation of its infernal dishonesty. He would go into someone's house—under the already-dishonest pretense of being a "struggling college student" who didn't really give a hoot in hell whether he sold any vacuum cleaners—and begin a basic demonstration, laboring because of the missing hand, which slowed everything down, until his supervisor showed up. This was Salesman Number Two, the Master, who came in under the guise of coincidentally being "in the neighborhood" looking for Jerome.

The Master went for the jugular, attempting to overcome the customer's every objection to buying the expensive appliance, while Jerome looked on in abject and embarrassed silence. It was a shameful thing, pure black comedy. Well, he thought, it's a job. Not much of a job, but better than nothing, at any rate.

And then he decided to head home, although he did not know where he was. He did an abrupt about-face, headed back toward the woods, and attempted to make his way straight back the way he had come. He walked on and on, his mind now gone mercifully blank, and he did not find his way back until well after dark.

CHAPTER TWENTY-THREE

MARIA HAD VERY few co-workers. In fact, she knew no one she could truly call a co-worker, no one who provided daily or consistent contact. Her supervisor was rarely around, and she had no need to see him on a regular basis. His primary role was to review her patient reports and, unless there was a problem, she had no use for him. The other therapists, though around occasionally, gave her little help and little trouble. Their jobs, like hers, involved going from patient to patient, and although they sometimes crossed paths in the break room, they'd all adjusted long ago to solitude, independent and aloof like sculptors or painters.

But they saw the change in Maria, and it became a topic of conversation.

"You know, I hate to talk, but Maria—you know, pretty girl, long dark hair...?"

"Oh. Sure, I know who you mean."

"She's been acting kind of strange, don't you think?"

"How so?"

"Well, she never used to work overtime, and now she seems to be *volunteering* for it, for God's sake. Not only that, but —" and here the voice lowered, conspiratorial "— she's been awfully *serious*. She used to be smiling all the time. I hope everything is all right at home."

It was true. Where there was always a warm smile before, there was a set jaw, and two lines like small crescent moons had formed at the corners of her mouth. Her eyes, when she came into the room—oblivious to the conversation—looked like those of someone who has been through surgery recently, or is deep in mourning.

In unison, the women said, "Hi, Maria."

She smiled feebly. "Hi."

They exchanged knowing glances across the table. "Say, Maria, what are you doing tonight after work? Carol and I were talking about drinks at Fitzie's."

"I'll have to take a rain check. I've been going walking after work, for exercise, and that's taking up a lot of my time."

"Really? How far do you walk?"

"I'm not sure. Probably seven or eight miles. It takes about two hours."

"Seven miles! I could never do that, I'll bet I couldn't even do one," said Carol.

At this, Maria brightened. "It's not bad. It's good cardio, and it keeps me out of trouble." And with that, she got a juice from the vending machine. "See you later," she said as she passed.

"Take care," they replied.

And she did go out walking that night, just as she said, and to blank herself out, she repeated song lyrics in her head:

Promises as empty as the tear that never dries,
Promises as empty as the cloudless summer skies....

She told herself that she would allow no tears to form in the corners of her eyes. She felt no sadness: only a void that she tried, again and again, to fill with the fleeting balm of oxygen.

Eventually, though, her thoughts turned to Jerome Brothers. She refused to let him rent space in her head, but for just a moment, the thought made an almost welcome intrusion into the void inside her. She walked on, and remembered how insistently he had tried to get her to "open up" to him one night. It was the first night they had made love—a day or two after the first futile attempt—and they had been walking slowly together beneath the oaks on Temblan Street.

"Tell me," he had said, over and over. "Tell me about Maria Santisia. Tell me about the moss-covered rocks near the river where you used to walk, or the butterfly that landed on your fingertip, or the nightsweats you had when you were seven and had a bad fever. Tell me about the first *crush* you had."

She'd laughed, and he'd laughed with her. They were able to joke then with a comfortable intimacy that was almost alarming, considering they'd met only several weeks before. It was like a summer romance, achingly beautiful and—adolescent. Damn it all, it *was* adolescent. And the thought made her want to banish him from her mind completely.

She walked on, the lyrics in her head fusing with that single, insistent, immutable phrase: "Tell me."

And then, mercifully, she blocked it all out, drowned it, with deep, deep breaths of healing oxygen.

"It is not when I am going to meet him, but when I am just turning away and leaving him alone, that I discover that God is. I say, God. I am not sure that that is the name. You will know what I mean."

—Thoreau

CHAPTER TWENTY-FOUR

ED ROBBINS WAS alone again.

Thursday night, and Margaret was working late again. So, he thought, here we go, and hoisted a bottle of Miller with defiance.

He swallowed, sighing deeply down into himself. He touched the match to the cigarette and settled back into the sofa in preparation for a night of television. He propped his frizzy head up on pillows, his mouth curled into the wet sneer of someone who has suffered, bewildered and peevish, for a long time. As always, he thought of Margaret, thought of her the way he had been thinking of her for quite some time: the *bitch*. All she did was nag at him, or try to guilt-trip him. She was sad, he knew, felt life had cheated her, because his luck had been rotten. It was almost unbelievable, what she'd become.

He thought of her late hours, her neglectful, and neglected, dinners, her strident voice. What a royal bitch. Then suddenly, with the power of a small explosion in his head, he saw that she was right, and that her suffering was undeserved. He saw it all, saw it as if through the painful clarity of sobriety.

For even on days when he was relatively dry, his perception had not been clear. But now he felt touched with some kind of momentary intuition, second sight. He saw himself stretched like a fat dog on the hammock in the backyard, saw himself staring glumly over lakes and streams and rivers, saw Margaret trying with the resilience born of desperation to make ends meet for them both, saw her watching, with waning compassion, his inevitable dissipation.

And, as if reduced to an emotional infant by this glimpse of the truth, he began to blubber. His mouth stretched across his teeth, and he wept hideously, choking up great sobs of grief, not just for Margaret but for himself, too, for their spent life. He knew he looked pathetic, could see himself in the mirror on the opposite wall. And still he blubbered heartily, guzzling his beer in huge gulps when the sobs subsided, stubbing out his cigarette with sweaty fingers. He cried for Margaret, and for himself, and when he was done, he sat immobile and stared at himself, a drained and deflated lump with the eyes of a dead man.

When Margaret walked in and found him like that, she was sure he had gone into a catatonic stupor of some kind. She was not far from the truth: he was in a state of unutterable apathy, and he knew it. He simply did not care what happened, anywhere, to her or to him, or the world, for that matter. At that moment, the universe could have come to a blazing end, and he would have sat there, numb with disbelief and dispassion, staring at the television.

"Ed," she said.

He did not stir.

She waited a moment. Calm, it seemed. Something almost frightening flashed in her eyes, as if the color had receded, and faint beads of perspiration appeared on her forehead.

"Ed," she repeated. "You're naht —" she hesitated. "Are you all right?"

Nothing at first, the darkness of all their years suddenly between them. He blinked once, hard, breathed in the silence slowly, and as he did so, all the clarity of the previous half hour receded, swept away as his mind slammed its curtain of denial back down into place, implacable.

He sighed softly. "I'm fine," he said. "How was your day?"

She stood directly before him, looking hard, and for a moment, he saw only the receding gleam in her eye, shimmering for just an instant more in that long suspiration.

"I had a great day. Fabulous." The sarcasm in her tone made her cringe back before she paused and smiled. "Would you like to hear abowt it?" She sounded as if she was speaking to a child.

"Sure. Yeah, sure." He shifted in his seat, visibly uncomfortable.

"Well, to begin with, I got an excellent report this morning from my supervisor's supervisor." She launched into a long list of the day's accomplishments and setbacks, frustrations and triumphs.

Feigning interest, his attention span stretched to the breaking point, he faded in and out of the monologue, which became curiously surreal. His jaw grew slack, and he felt his eyes glaze over as she spoke. With an inward sigh of disgust, she realized she would be unsurprised to see a droplet of drool form on that pendulous underlip.

When she finished—only a little frustrated by the knowledge that Ed had absorbed an unknown, if miniscule, quantity of what she'd told him—she sat down quickly, all in one motion, like a small child who has just completed a recital. Her hands folded themselves in her lap, and she looked down at them for a moment before glancing up at him, indomitable, an unspoken question on her lips.

"And what did *you* do today?" she said finally.

She dreaded asking, dreaded his answer. She tried to keep the accusatory tone from creeping into her voice, tried to calm herself as she prepared for his answer. It was slow in coming, as if he was trying to remember or, more likely, trying to come up with something truly original, if not honest, and so she gazed steadily somewhere beyond him, thinking comforting thoughts of pastel colors, cool healing waters, breezes of summer oceans.

"Naht much," he said.

How anticlimactic, she thought.

"I didn't feel that great," he continued. "And, uh, I'm kinda depressed, Margaret."

Strange, she thought, he hasn't called me that in a long time.

"I don't know," he said, "it's such a rat race, you know? Lookin' for a jahb. And you know what the goddamn jahb market's like now. I don't know. I'll try tomorrow, hon, okay?"

Hon. He hadn't called her that in a long time, either.

She began to get up. "This place —" she tossed a hand in the air, a gesture vaguely theatrical, and despairing "— this place is such a *mess.*"

It was true: old newspapers lay stacked on the sofa where he'd left them, remnants of the past several days scattered about the room. In the kitchen, a bag of empty bottles spilled out of a corner and almost into the next room. Shoes, dirt, dust, and pieces of lint adorned the floor in patches, and there was a smell of slightly stale onions.

"I know," he said, getting up unsteadily. "I'm sorry. I'll clean up tomorrow before I go owt to jahb-hunt. It's just—I dunno."

She watched him as he picked things up absently. He took a pile of newspapers from the sofa and moved them to the chair, a pointless gesture. And she followed him silently as he went into the kitchen and began washing the dishes piled up in the sink. She stood at a distance, her arms folded across her chest. He did not turn toward her as he spoke.

"I know you're under a laht of stress, Margie. Christ, believe me, I know. And you're doin' a hell of a jahb, you really are. It's just that—well, y'know, with the jahb market bein' the way it is, and feelin' the way I been feelin' with this damned change in the weather...."

Still she was silent, as he went on about what a difficult summer it had been. She seemed to be listening down into herself, tapping some reservoir of power from which she had been previously unable to draw. With something almost like pride, and certainly with a good deal of determination in her voice, she said, "Ed."

"Hmm?"

"Ed, I think you should go for cownseling." Her face mask-like, expressionless.

"Cownseling? What for?" He recoiled a bit.

"Well, for starters, you don't seem to have much motivation. You —"

"*I'm* naht th—"

"Let me finish," she commanded. He shrugged, began drying the dishes. "You don't seem to have much motivation; you don't seem to really *want* to work —" he made a gesture of protest "— wait, I'm not done yet. You're naht in a great frame of mind most of the time. Now, if you want me to go see a therapist with you, that's fine—I'll go. But if naht, then I think you should go yourself." She drew herself up, as if prepared for a rebuttal. "And that's all I have to say. Except for one more thing." She held her hand up, like she expected him to argue. "I think you should do it as soon as possible. Things aren't getting better." She folded her arms.

He stood silently, gently scrubbing the pan with a circular motion, as though trying to wear a hole in it. "I can understand where you're coming from," he said. "I know it's been kinda tough for ya, and I know you're under a laht of stress, but okay. If you wanna go for cownseling, I'll go. I don't care. I don't believe in any of that stuff, Margie, you know that. But if it'll make you happy, I'll go. I don't care."

Her eyes relaxed, and she smiled a tiny little smile, barely discernible. A smile of triumph. "Okay," she said simply, turning to go out, then pivoted back. "I'm going upstairs to take a bath before I eat anything."

"Okay," he said.

She tripped lightly up the stairs. The whole house seemed to glow with some weird electricity, and her face felt flushed with excitement. She walked into the bathroom, closed the door, and said, "Yes" under her breath, her fists clenched in victory. Then she drew water for her bath, and disrobed slowly.

When she lay back in the tub, hot water loosened her tense shoulders ever so slightly, and the whole world seemed to drop away. She saw them, herself and Ed, with the clarity of a detached observer, and everything was all right. She had won.

And yet it felt like a hollow victory. She had managed to get him to cave in, but how far would it go, how much good would it do? What if he really didn't care? And what if counseling proved futile as a result? What if he sat there, apathetic and sullen, a brick wall of obstinacy and contempt, like an atheist at Sunday morning services?

She knew it was ridiculous to look that far ahead, and she tried to forget about it as she shifted into a more comfortable position. She lathered her legs with the bath soap, pressing her strong fingers firmly against the flesh of her thighs and drawing them upward. She sighed quietly at the almost unfamiliar stirring within her and closed her eyes, leaning her head back against the tiles, rubbing soap into a thick lather around her calves and ankles.

CHAPTER TWENTY-FIVE

IT WAS LATE autumn in Carverville, but it might just as well have been February. The weather grew mercilessly cold, the iron-grey bitterness of a New York winter, and the ground outside turned brittle as shale. Jerome Brothers sat and stared at his coffee pot, wondering whether a watched pot ever does boil.

It was cold in the house, too—had been, off and on, ever since last winter, when the furnace went on the blink. He decided to turn the thermostat up and sauntered out into the adjacent hallway, cup in hand. But as occasionally happened, he forgot he did not have a free hand, and so he had to bend to set the empty cup slowly down on the brown carpet and straighten back up to adjust the small clear dial. It was already set at sixty-eight, but the place felt fifty-eight, and he cranked it up past seventy, muttering, "Screw the electric bill."

When he returned to the kitchen, he poured himself a steaming cup of coffee and added two teaspoonsful of sugar. A bit spilled due to the relative lack of dexterity with his left hand. He stirred it slowly, let the gentle swirling motion soothe him like a whirlpool.

His thoughts turned to Maria. Damned if she hadn't been right, and damned if that wasn't, in itself, the most intolerable aspect of the situation. He wanted to find a way to alleviate the pain, but he did not drink or use drugs, exercise was a grind, food a mere necessity, and sex, a fond, though distant, memory. There was only Maria, himself, and the indomitable distance between them. It had no face, and offered no solace.

Maria. Her name sang like the title of some well loved song, nostalgic as the sound of crickets and nightingales, redolent with the warmth of something fantastic and indefinable. Time, too, softened the blow, although it had not yet healed his wound.

He remembered the first time she came to the house, how she invested it with a kind of magical warmth. She'd only been there for a few hours, accumulated over a period of several days, and yet—as if she'd always been there—he still saw her leaning against the counter in her wrinkly turquoise blouse—the one with the big pockets that she wore with a black gabardine skirt—laughing at the foolish things he'd said under her spell.

I'd look at you that way if I were a three-headed iguana.

She was sexy, sexy in the way that a much younger woman would be, full of the vitality of uncorrupted youth. And although he remembered her that way, he remembered, too, what she had been like in the midst of an argument: she had grown cold, then vicious. Then hysterical. And then gone.

Thinking about it was strange. A precarious feeling adheres to such a brief and fragile relationship, not unlike the sense that accompanies the change from ownership of a house to renting an apartment, the feeling that one is walking about in a building that could tumble down at any moment. And that seemed an appropriate analogy, he thought, since the brief thing that flared up between them had crashed down before it was even complete. He did not want to think about it any longer, and he tried to push the subject from his mind while he drank his coffee.

But when he succeeded in blanking himself out, nothing remained to think about, and so he tried to focus on that nothingness. He stood to move out of the room, then simply walked back into the adjacent hallway, where he paced absentmindedly in front of the painting on the wall. An odd picture, a frumpy-looking thing, it had been there when he moved into the house. It always reminded him of his aunt and uncle, although it was nothing more than a pair of oversized panda bears in an unlikely field of daisies. He laughed a little and wondered if he'd kept the painting out of some misguided sense of loyalty.

He realized how ridiculous he must look pacing in front of the pandas, with his stumpy arm and his coffee. Yet he felt consoled, almost elated, for he knew that, even as he marched in his own house like some maimed soldier on a coffee break, somewhere a glorious plan was being drawn up for him.

That knowledge came to him with a shock, as a thought for which he was not only not responsible, but also of which he could not help being justifiably suspicious. More than that, he felt incredulous, and a little afraid. He went into the kitchen, dumped out his coffee, then decided to take a shower. It was Saturday, and he had nothing to do, but a shower felt necessary nonetheless.

Even after all this time, showers were a challenge. Though his left arm was not particularly flexible at first, it had grown quite flexible during the past two months. He could reach most of his back if he had to, although it was only essential to reach the shoulders and upper back.

The main problem was unscrewing the shampoo bottle, which was usually already wet by the time he tried to pick it up. He had to remind himself to open the shampoo before turning on the water, so he could grip it snugly in the crook of his arm, without it slipping out. He'd lost large blobs of shampoo as a result of this problem.

Even the shower was not so bad. The post-shower routine of wielding a toothbrush and shaving with a razor, though, proved grueling. He found himself switching back and forth between an electric and a straight razor, each of which had severe disadvantages. With the electric razor, his heavy beard got a superficial shave, but he found the straight razor difficult to hold left-handed, which made it frightening to use.

And he had grown to hate brushing his teeth: putting the toothbrush down on the back part of the sink, unscrewing the toothpaste tube, squeezing toothpaste carefully onto the bristles while trying not to knock the brush over. Perhaps worst of all was the knowledge that all this exercise made his left arm bigger and stronger, while the unused arm began to wither away like an old tree branch. He wondered if Maria would have given him exercises for the arm if she'd stuck around.

He thought of the Robbinses while he stood there brushing. It was strange that Ed Robbins leapt into his mind; he hadn't seen Ed or Margaret in quite some time, and he had no idea what or how they were doing. He'd been friendly with them since before his aunt and uncle died, and kept in touch with them periodically, though their correspondence was haphazard at best.

For his own part, he'd called once in those past three years, while they exchanged Christmas cards with him. Beyond that, they'd only run into each other five or six times during those first crucial months after his aunt and uncle's deaths, and, of course, they'd sent a card after his accident. He thought about calling them, maybe to see if they wanted to get together, maybe just to see how they were.

It was strange, he thought, that he hadn't even run into them at Macy's Market, or farther down along Chestnut Avenue. It was a small town, after all. He put off calling them, for that day at any rate, but he wondered where Ed was hiding himself.

"Your joy is your sorrow unmasked."

— KAHLIL GIBRAN

CHAPTER TWENTY-SIX

MARIA WAS WALKING down the road, walking, walking, steadily and with determination, and in her head rang the lyrics of an old hymn (SPEEEEEAK LORD, I LONG TO LISTEN TO YOUR VOOOICE), and she went with it, let it run through her mind like a mantra. As she moved, she concentrated on her breathing, and on the way her pounding feet broke up each word into several syllables by if she sang aloud (SPEE-EE-EE-EE-EE-EAK LO-O-O-O-O-ORD), and although the idea seemed funny enough to make her laugh out loud, it was also suddenly very unfunny.

A feeling followed her, a feeling of emptiness, and she'd been trying to fill it with everything within her grasp: bingeing on TV sitcoms and M&Ms, talking to her cat Rasputin, cleaning everything in sight, calling old acquaintances to surprise them. But of course, she recognized the emptiness at the core of it all, connecting it with Jerome Brothers. She felt angry, and she felt guilty about being angry, and yet the feeling only kept building. She fought to push it all away, ashamed of the fear and guilt, and that, in turn, made her angrier.

She was angry at God, and empty, and dead inside. Why in hell would a just God, a loving and good and kind God, let this happen to her, or, worse yet, do this to her? And still that mantra careened through her head (SPEEEEEEAK LORD, I LONG TO LISTEN TO YOUR VOOOIICE), and she could never get through the song, always returning to that beginning line, filled with the urgency of hoped-for reacquaintance, as if reopening a book she'd been reading, returning to and even rereading part of the left-hand page and beginning again (SPEEEEEAK LORD), and still her feet went up and down, up and down, her breathing regular, and noisy, like the chugging of a washing machine.

It was late, nearly nine o clock. She'd gotten home at five, eaten a frozen dinner, given herself until nearly seven to let it digest, filling the time with household chores, dishwashing, laundry, changing the cat's litterbox. Then she'd begun the walk, the daily grind that exhausted her enough for sleep to come when eleven o'clock rolled around.

She checked her watch: 8:55. She was almost home now, and glad of it. Her lips were parched, her feet pounding pavement, it seemed, for too long tonight. The blood hammered in her head, and the intrusion of lyrics, and of the memory of Jerome Brothers, was almost welcome, a paradox beyond her reckoning, but soothing, like cool water (SPEEEAK LORD), and somehow better.

In the most active part of her mind, the part suspended above the core of breathing and the calm opiate high of endorphin-flow, she thought of Jerome, thought seriously, and in terms of their early meeting and romance. It was okay, she thought. It really was. Not perfect, but he was a nice guy after all. The way his eyes looked in the hospital when we first met. Why? And that damned *laugh*. He was funny. She saw he was in so much pain and just wanted to help. She would have done anything to take care of him. Professionalism. How could she have done more? She didn't overstep any boundaries; she did what she was supposed to do. To a point. But then: that kiss. And all the rest of that, damn it.

God, it's cold out here. Dark. It gets darker every day now.

She remembered a time when she'd been at the mall with her mother and grandmother. She'd been nine or ten. A little boy was running along past the shops, and he passed Maria and her guardians at a jog, his hard-soled shoes smacking the stone floor with a steady *thwap thwap*. And suddenly he fell, in slow motion it seemed, his close-cropped head disappearing as his small rear end bucked into the air. He struck his knees before his torso slapped against the stone, and Maria's mother and grandmother gasped, recoiling.

But Maria was at his side instantly, helping him to his feet, ignoring his tears with disinterested politeness, stroking and patting the nape of his neck with reassurances that it was "all right, all right." The scene was touching to passersby—and especially to her mother and grandmother—but Maria knew the truth: somewhere beneath her facade of calm caretaker, for just a moment before the boy could stand solidly, she felt a powerful contempt, and a desire to punish. She felt the pull of the sadist within, and only the fear of being punished by her mother and grandmother, and a recognition of the hideous impropriety, restrained her from shoving him, from kicking his bruises, or, at the very least, loudly proclaiming his stupidity at having been so clumsy.

She hadn't thought of the boy, or of her grandmother and mother, for a long time. Strange how, lately, she'd remembered certain isolated, irrelevant incidents from the distant past, as if her mind roamed back among memories while unable to focus on present problems. "This is your life," she thought, grimly ironic.

And then she felt, for a moment, like a child bursting from a pile of leaves, and after that sudden, shocking buoyancy, she felt confused. It was crazy, yet the mood swing seemed to have an inscrutable logic of its own. For a moment, everything was so clear, the unity and harmony of all things, the connections among her and other people, the rhythmic ebb and flow, the heft of experience. Everything seemed clear. Then anger boiled back up, swamped her, like a wave crashing down on itself, with fear and guilt and terrifying loneliness and claustrophobia, and finally, a desperation so profound it threatened to smother her.

On and on she walked, and, as the apartments came into view, she felt a little freer, as if some avenue of escape was at least possible. The deathlike sensation of guilt and desperation left her slightly more numb than before, but she felt anger just beneath the surface, coming out in short breaths, making the pain in her calves and ankles more and more welcome. The sky was filling with grey, moonlit clouds as she neared home, and wind was blowing through the trees with a soulful and elegiac sound. She'd grown thoughtful as she neared the apartments, the fear and desperation had ebbed away, and she saw a glimmer of hope beneath that mass of unresolved emotions.

When she was finally inside and sitting on the sofa, still breathing heavily, it suddenly occurred to her to call her friend Toni Myers. Another strange surprise, this sudden thought of Toni—she hadn't seen or spoken to her for many months. That's weird, she thought. What made me think of her?

It was as strange as the thought of the boy in the mall, but she went with intuition and called. At first, the sound on the other end was muffled, ringing like an inevitably bad connection, but she resisted the temptation to hang up and redial. And when the line clicked, there was Toni's voice, bright and reassuring: "Hello-o?"

"Toni, hi. This is Maria."

"Mari—Santisia?"

"Yeah."

"How are you?" She sounded amazed, and pleased.

"Okay, how are you?" asked Maria.

"Good. Oh, this is so *weird....*"

"What? What's weird?"

"Well, I was just thinking about you. In fact, Oscar and I were just talking about you."

"Really?" She pursed her lips. Why were they talking about her?

"Yeah. He was saying, 'What ever happened to that friend of yours, Maria? You know, the cute brunette?'"

"Get outta here...."

"I'm serious. He was busting my ass, but still—isn't that *weird?*"

"I was just walking along, and all of a sudden, I thought of calling you. It must be fate. When was the last time I ran into you?"

"Oh God," Toni laughed. "What's this, November?"

"Almost December. Exactly. I thought, well, why not? There must be some reason for doing it, since it popped into my head that way, even if it is just to say hello."

"Well, I'm glad you called. How is everything?"

"Okay." For the first time, Maria knew for certain that was a lie. She felt her face flush. "Well. Not bad."

"Yeah? Are ya okay?" Toni cleared her throat. "You sound like you've been running."

Maria laughed. "Oh, *that*. Walking, actually." Her heart slowed.

"Walking, eh? That's what I need, some good exercise."

"Yeah, it's great. Listen...." She paused.

"Yes?"

"I'm not really all that okay."

"No?"

"No."

"You didn't sound that okay, Maria."

"I didn't?"

"You sound like someone who's grieving...."

"Uh-oh, here we go."

"No, really. Your voice is hollow. Like someone who's lost a close relative. You know, 'Time to make the bed. Time to feed the kids. Hi, everything's fine. Time to wash the car.' You haven't had a death in the family, have you?" There was a sound of her dragging on a cigarette.

"No, not lately. Not since—hell, not since my dad died."

"That's good. So what's wrong?" She exhaled noisily.

"I don't know. I had a sort of aborted relationship, but..."

"Aaah."

"— that was a while ago. What? What is that, 'aaah?'"

"Well, that might have something to do with what you're sounding like."

"What am I sounding like?"

"Well, a minute ago you sounded like Robotic Maria, a clone of the real you. 'Maria-in-a-coma.' Now you sound like...well...."

"Like what?"

Toni paused. "Like you're pissed off."

"I'm not pissed off!"

"No, obviously you're in a state of blissful contentedness." There was a smile in her voice.

Maria laughed. "Well, okay. I'm not exactly jumping for joy, but I'm not angry with you."

"I didn't say 'with me.' I just meant in general."

"Don't psychoanalyze me, Toni."

"I'm not. I'm just suggesting a possibility. I promise."

"Well, okay. Listen, Toni..."

"Ye-e-e-es?"

"I don't know if I should ask you this—I mean, you being my friend and all...I don't want to put you on the spot."

"Go ahead, don't worry about putting me on the spot."

She took a deep breath. "Do you think I should go for counseling?" She held the rest of the breath, awaiting the reply.

"Well, I'm not really in a position to —"

"Oh, come on," she interrupted. "Don't dance around it, I can take the blow to the ego. We're *friends*, Toni."

"Maria, this really isn't like you. And it's so unexpected."

"What? What isn't like me?"

"Being this jumpy. I would say that, if for no other reason than the fact that you're extremely jumpy, you should at least *consider* some counseling."

"With you!?"

"I didn't say that!" Toni laughed. "Holy shit, you've gotta relax a little."

"You're right. You're right, you're right, you're right. I'm just feeling a little crazy, that's all. So, okay: where do I go from here? What do *you* suggest, *Dr.* Myers?" It was only a joke, but the similarity between it and her old "*Mr.* Brothers" was unmistakable, and she cringed.

"Well, I don't know if this would help, but I have a friend who practices a certain type of psychotherapy, sort of 'New Age,' I guess you'd call it —"

"Oookay...."

"— It deals with, uh, various issues from a perspective of—how do I say it?"

"Past-life regression?" Maria chuckled.

"No, no. Well, let me just ask you something: do you find yourself wanting to, or trying to, take care of other people's problems—to the detriment of taking care of yourself?"

"I don't know. Maybe. Yeah, in fact, I was just thinking about that earlier, and having had that impulse as a girl."

"Okay. Do you feel you're affected by other people's behavior?"

There was a pause.

Maria took a deep breath. "Of course. Isn't that *normal?*"

"Well, 'normal' is a problematic word—it has a lot of positive or negative connotations, plus it depends on the person. What's normal for one person may not be for you and me. But you know that. It's kind of like 'average.' I mean, nobody's really average."

"Mm-hm."

"One more thing," Toni said. "Do you ever feel responsible for other people's feelings, or reactions?"

She took a deeper breath this time.

"Yeah—yeah, I guess so. I guess I do. Why?"

"I think I know someone."

"Who is she?" asked Maria. "What's *her* deal?"

"Well, let's just say her primary focus is going back and sort of nurturing the little kid we all once were, that's still a part of us—if that makes sense."

"I thought that stuff was a lot of malarkey."

"No, it's not. Let me give you her number, instead of trying to confuse you. Her name is Madeline Page."

A final pause, in which Maria's world seemed to hang in the balance. Then, "Okay," and the tiniest part of the weight upon her lifted.

CHAPTER TWENTY-SEVEN

IN JOHNNY CARUSO'S bedroom, on the top shelf of a bookcase that served as shelving for his stereo speakers, stood a kind of mini-library that revealed to the astute observer that Johnny was not quite the philistine he seemed. In addition to copies of *The Red Badge of Courage* and *Huck Finn*, a well-thumbed *On The Road*, and an equally worn *Fear and Loathing in Las Vegas*, there were also copies of Nietzsche's *Thus Spoke Zarathustra, On the Genealogy of Morals* and *Ecce Homo*. There were books on psychology and sociology, a copy of William Glasserman's *Reality Therapy*, Roget's thesaurus, flanked by *Demian, The Sun Also Rises,* Hitler's *Mein Kampf,* and *No One Here Gets Out Alive*, the Jim Morrison biography. Hitler and Morrison were Johnny's heroes, neither from any particular anti-Semitism nor a reverence for the music of the Doors, although both would certainly apply. His fascination came instead from both Hitler's and Morrison's ability to mesmerize, and perhaps even control, massive crowds. For the same reason, Martin Luther King and Gandhi intrigued him, although they were far less alluring than Hitler and Morrison, or, for that matter, Mussolini. Johnny himself was paralyzed before groups if he had to address them.

He sat at the desk in the corner, a child's rolltop desk of the old-fashioned type. The top up, he hunched over a notebook, a pen in his hand, hair drooping down over his eyes, squinting like someone who has lost his glasses. He looked almost like a model with his long hair and angular body, but something in his eyes suggested corruption or insanity, anyone looking hard at him would have seen that just beneath that look there was an anger he was much too numb to even acknowledge, and beneath that an undeniable unbearable pain, a pain so excruciating and complete that, had he been able to feel a portion of it, the brain would have only been able to stand back and observe the outraged and guilt-corrupted flesh, awestruck and sorrowful.

He'd been out roaming the neighborhood earlier, hungrily searching like a wolf for he knew not what, and his nostrils were still filled with the rich nostalgic smell of dead leaves and the sharp odor of woodsmoke from neighborhood fires that had embedded themselves in his flannel shirt, and they mingled mysteriously with the aftertaste of whiskey in his throat, a taste that called up images of men around campfires blowing into cupped hands on a cold November night. None of which seemed connected to what he'd written on the page before him.

Why does the human race find itself so deeply entangled in superficiality? The extreme, ascetic rules of etiquette, concocted by a blind hierarchy, point an accusing finger at the man of reason. He will not be left alone with his reflections, but is instead shuffled and ridiculed, by these masters and mistresses of snobbery, this "upper" class. Man has never been satisfied with equality, and therefore resorts to the superficial slime of ascetic etiquette in an attempt to alienate the narcissists, the idealists, those of reason, passion, compassion, and philanthropy.

"To repress is to triumph," say these bastard offspring of convention. "To have wealth signifies 'status,' and denotes 'goodness.'"

This ignorant, shallow conclusion is instilled into the minds of babes born into wealth. They breed like worms in filthy swamps, this "other half." They have not yet felt the sting of the scorpion, the heel of the iron boot that will crush their skulls. They poison the minds of their children with castrating laws, and blind cruel rules. They are the wealthy, have always been the wealthy, and they brand their children with the same evil wounds they themselves are festering.

There is no solution to this problem, no way to free the caged identities of the nouveaux riche who carry a silver spoon in their clutching fingers as they emerge from the womb. They will live and grow in an artificial paradise, finding satisfaction only in the superficial. Even we men of reason and passion, lords of power and grace, will do nothing to save them from their journey on the money-littered road to Hell.

He smiled, satisfied. There did not seem to be anything to add, and he sat back, thinking.

Louise. Lou-ee-eeeeze? Wake up. Ya f—no, no, sorry: ya effin bitch. Can't say that word in your house. Ya effin *bitch*! Ha.

He leaned forward again. What was it Nietzsche had said? He grabbed his copy of *On the Genealogy of Morals* and flipped through it almost frantically, until he found the well-marked page.

"Tourists...They climb mountains like animals, stupid and sweating; one has forgotten to tell them that there are beautiful views on the way up."

That's it, he thought. She's like a damn tourist. Stupid and sweating. He cackled hideously.

He wanted to be a philosopher, had wanted to be one for a long time, since before he'd even heard of Nietzsche. But when he had read Nietzsche, he'd felt the mourning feeling—both awe-struck and deadening—the useless, hopeless feeling that all that could be done had been done, all that could be said, said well. And thinking now about his life, he despaired, until anger came up into his throat like bile, a rage so fierce it could pick him up like a toy in a whirlwind and carry him away, he could feel it, a wind blowing clean through, cancelling everything that resembled fear or remorse. His eyebrow flickered.

Jesus, he said to himself. What kind of a dirtbag am I? I know I'm mean—I'm the meanest motherfucker I know—but I didn't know I was *that* mean. I could kill. I mean really kill. Imagine it. The blood. The screams fading on the wind. Power. Unbelievable, what that would feel like. What *would* that feel like? Like a parade? Like Sunday school?

He laughed out loud. Like a fucking *prom*?!

Wow. He slumped back. *I gotta cut this out. This isn't even funny anymore. But it just sounds right. It sounds like something that, if I could do it, would be like a first step—into a new way of life. I could be, like, the leader of a militia or a vigilante group or somethin'. If I could do this first, just get over that first hurdle. I'd need a plan.*

There were endless possibilities, it seemed: rape, murder, kidnapping, armed robbery. He thought about horrendous acts of violence he could commit, and then, guilt-ridden, he thought about what it would be like to die a violent death. Though almost incredibly funny when applied to someone else, the notion of being killed by someone himself was an outrage. It would be one thing if he were to kill himself; that was entirely different than being murdered. Suicide was a decision, the result of a whole series of steps, the last being hopelessness, in many cases. He knew that.

He ran a hand through his hair and scratched the back of his neck, as if he had a deep and terrible itch that would not yield. He tapped his foot against the leg of the chair persistently, soon growing numb with the effect. It was like some narcotic, this tapping. Like the trembling and quaking of an akathisiac. It seemed to come from some deep, uncontrollable force within, and would have been terrible to see, had there been anyone there to see it.

But there was no one, he was alone in that unkempt room, as truly alone as only the suffering can be. It was as if the sky closed over him, folded him and his tiny room into the unforgiving earth. And with rage he thought of his mother again: the bitch. *She's like all the rest of 'em. Try'na "take care of me." Try'na put on a big show for everybody. "Now, young man, don't you dare use that language on* me." *Fuckin' joke. I could rip 'er up, man. I could turn her into lawn mulch. Yeah. Great.* Then *what? Who the fuck am I supposed to live with then? Dweeper? Jeez-us! I gotta get my mind off this.*

He rummaged around for a CD, sifting through piles of dirty clothes, tossing empty beer cans and pairs of underwear across the room. At last, he found the disc he wanted and put it on. It was the Hatchet Boys song "Underground":

Doom and destruction
In the underground
Cold-hearted screamin'
Is our favorite sound...
We're gonna drag her
To the underground,
We're gonna give 'er her due:
She's gonna rock the beams
With her screams,
We're gonna make her black and blue.

He played a vicious air guitar, smacking his hand against his thigh with each chord. A well-known song, one he could have sung in his sleep, as familiar as the theme song of *I Love Lucy* or the smell of death. His eyes were closed tightly, and his mane of curly blond hair shook down over them again and again, like a shaman. When he opened his eyes after the song had finally finished, the look in them was almost beatific.

CHAPTER TWENTY-EIGHT

JEROME SAT IN his house, leaned back against the rattled old TV set, its cool smooth veneer comforting against his back, and put his hand over his head. When the feeling came upon him, it was almost like a dizzy spell, and a certain amount of blood had gone to his head. He sighed deep down into himself, and a feeling of inexpressible sadness came over him, a poignancy and vulnerability almost buoyant enough to lift him up even as it made him want to cry out loud. He longed to stand in the sun and hold himself against the wind and weep unabashedly, like a child whose favorite stuffed animal has been torn apart and discarded by a parent. But he could not muster even a tear.

It was Sunday, and the week had been hellish. No compelling reason to expect the approaching week to be better. Work was a nightmare, a ghastly joke. He'd sold nothing, not even an "attachment replacement," and his refrigerator was quickly emptying, but he knew he could do no more than get up and give it "another hundred and ten percent" tomorrow. Jesus, he thought, I hate that expression.

On the job, he had been told, again and again, that there were two types of people in the world: winners and losers. He had always winced inwardly and rejected the smarmy cliché, but he'd begun to feel the seductive pull of its so-called logic. He had lost his hand. He was losing at his job. And he had lost Maria, if in fact she had ever been his. He'd become one of the losers.

He stood and looked out the window. A peculiar quality to the light that day seemed to play on his weaknesses, the sky the color of skim milk at the bottom of a bowl of cereal, the sun barely visible behind the haze, and not quite spherical. That impulse to stand in the sun and cry like a baby mingled with the most forceful repudiation, and he named the feeling in his heart as weakness and cast it aside in defiance.

There would be no more Marias, no more hellish weeks, no more unsuccessful jobs. The will to conquer, succeed, destroy adversity—a survival instinct taken to the *nth* degree—would sustain him, carrying him through to the end. No matter what, he said quietly to himself while the light rang down through a crack in the clouds, transfixing him there.

He had never been terribly close to any one woman. On some level he had loved, but it had been defiantly adolescent, and he knew it. He had dated and, in a sense, grew closer to some people than he had been able to get to Maria. But it had been different with her. He'd felt something, an almost religious awe that made him stand back and take a long hard look at himself. Undeniably, the situation caused intolerable pain, which was a bit much, he thought, at this age. Imagine if it had gone on longer.

Somehow, he felt sure he would see her again, although he could not say why, but this interim period of solitude was almost unbearable. He felt terribly lonely, he admitted, yet he hadn't decided upon a course of action. Perhaps they could be friends again, although most likely not at this point.

What if she called him? The prospect was absurd, a near-impossibility, but he had to admit that it was possible. He would stammer and hem and haw if she called, that much he knew.

Maybe I should call her instead, and beat her to it, he thought. Maybe I should say the hell with it. Date other women. Perhaps an apology is in order. It would be horribly difficult to apologize, and he considered putting it off for another day at least. And while he was thinking about calling her, at the moment he decided not to, the phone rang. The sound, abrupt and deafening, startled his heart into a momentary thump, like a fist knocking at the walls of his ribcage. He froze.

"Oh, man," he breathed, heading for the phone. He paused and tapped his chest with his open palm, made sure all was still working inside. "Hello?"

"Jerome? Jerome Brothers?" A male.

He did not recognize the voice at first. "Yeah?"

"Heh-hey," the voice cajoled, "Jerry, man, this is Johnny. Johnny Caruso."

Oh God. "How's it going, Johnny? Everything O.K. at home?" He allowed himself this brief lapse into malice.

"Ah, swell, Jer, real swell. How's the *stump* doin'?"

The question stunned him, appalling not only for its lack of tact, but because of its ambiguity. Did Johnny mean the arm itself, or was he actually punning on it, referring to Jerome as The Stump? He decided to ignore the latter possibility.

"Well, I'm adjusting as best I can, John. So what can I do for ya?"

"Oh, I dunno. Just called to see what was up."

"Well, I'm just getting some things done around here," Jerome said.

"Wanna hang out later? Maybe look for bimbettes?"

Jesus. "No, thanks. No, I think I'll just pack it in early tonight."

"Okay, man. Hey, listen, Jer?"

"Yeah?"

"Sorry about the 'stump' thing. Really," his voice toneless.

Jerome almost chuckled. "Don't worry about it, Johnny," he told him, relieved to have cleared the air. "It wasn't your fault, kid. Nobody put me up in that tree, and besides, who'da thought...? Well, anyway, I don't wanna think about it."

"I know, it's just that —"

"Johnny."

He paused. "Yo."

"Forget it, kid."

"Okay, man." He sounded shaken.

"Okay?" Jerome repeated. It was almost a taunt.

"Okay."

"See ya 'round, Caruso."

"Later."

He hung up the phone. It was Sunday, a day of rest, and he was overtired. He had absolutely nothing he had to do, a daunting number of things he should be doing, and nothing he wanted to do. He turned on the TV and stared at a football game, his mind blank, while the little men with square shoulders and round multi-colored heads smashed against one another, again and again, soldiers on a battlefield. He lay there, half-crazed with a hunger he could not satiate, and let the yearning grow and feed upon itself, forgetting the dubious gift of self-knowledge that no longer sustained him.

CHAPTER TWENTY-NINE

ALTHOUGH LOUISE CARUSO knew there was something seriously wrong with her son, she felt that it would somehow be a reflection on her if she admitted this to anyone. She told herself there was nothing she could do, which showed a remarkable perspicacity on her part, but helped no one. Worst of all, she determined to continue what she'd been doing: hoping lamely for a change, relinquishing even the illusion of control, and accepting that she would live in fear until he no longer lived at the house, possibly even longer. At the bottom of it, as anyone could have seen from the slight tic she was developing (if not from the near-permanent contraction of her eyebrows), she was guilt-ridden.

Though no direct connection existed between her instinctive prudery and her blatant disapproval of Johnny's exploits, she tried to convince herself it was so, and while she could not help seeing him in her mind's eye, in a series of drunken and profligate indiscretions, she gritted her teeth and pushed those thoughts away. Boys will, after all, be boys. Was she just being "old-fashioned?"

But the thought of Ed Robbins, and what she saw him doing to himself and to poor Margaret, served as a constant intrusion, and it took a small leap of logic from the figure of Johnny at eighteen to that of Ed at forty-one. Picturing Johnny as another Ed Robbins, her fear and guilt solidified, and with them came resolve. Something had to be done.

Some revolutions take place around gleaming conference tables; others in the rice paddy itself. This one took place in the quiet of an afternoon in November, where the tiny old woman—for she was old now, far older than her years—gazed unseeing past the gauzy yellow curtains of her kitchen window. Most of the leaves were gone now, the sky had taken on the smoky, almost luminescent quality of a waking dream.

What to do, what to do. It was a weighty problem, and she felt underqualified. There was no one she could talk to, as far as she knew, and the realization intensified her helplessness. She ticked off the obvious candidates in her mind: Jerome? No, too close to the situation, and a friend to Johnny besides. *Obviously* not Margaret—she had enough of a booze battle in her own backyard. One of Johnny's other friends? No, she knew none of them well enough to approach, and it might prove disastrous to even attempt it.

She could not think of even a remote possibility other than Bill and Elaine McCullough. Elaine was a teacher; maybe she dealt with this kind of thing. And Bill? Well, he was all right. A nice guy. Perhaps he could be helpful too, in some way, though how exactly she did not know.

She decided to take a walk in the yard. It was late afternoon, and Johnny had not come home yet, which was all right with her. She stood and looked at the elm tree across the street. A radiant yellow, she had not noticed it until today: part of that was perhaps the simple fact that the sun was going down, and shining full upon the elm, lending it a fervent beauty that was almost painful. There was something somber, yet hopeful, about it. Louise was surprised and pleased by the hope this elm tree seemed to be holding out to her. She heard an airplane overhead, and, looking up, saw the white streak of a jet that had just traversed the sky, almost from horizon to horizon.

She hoped. If only he would change, or leave of his own volition. If only he would decide he had to stop hurting her the way he did, or at least recognize that that was what he was doing. Somehow the blazing yellow elm across the way was holding out some small vestige of hope for her, reaching out with friendly arms. It was fortunate that she had this last shred of hope, for the revolution she'd had in her head was already over. She'd even forgotten the possibility of calling Bill and Elaine, lapsing back into the feeble inertia which was almost comfortable by now. And as she went back into the house she was humming a snatch of some long-forgotten tune, her mind blank as an early morning blackboard.

The development of revolvers began officially in 1836, when Samuel Colt patented a rotating breach pistol with several chambers. Within the next fifteen years, the design was brought into common use.

In modern pistol-shooting, handguns may be used for pistol target matches. The typically favored calibers are the .22, the .38, and the .45. Each contestant usually fires ten slow-fire shots from fifty yards, ten timed-fire from twenty-five yards, and ten rapid-fire, also from twenty-five yards.

— FROM THE "STRAFFORD GUIDE TO HANDHELD FIREARMS"

CHAPTER THIRTY

THE SUN WAS already gone, and shards of rust-colored and purplish cloud scattered across the horizon as Bill McCullough drove home from work. He eased the big blue Olds up the on-ramp, accelerating as several cars passed him, looking for space on route seventeen.

It was November now, November the eighth, to be precise, and although October was gone and he'd made it past the anniversary of Joey's death, something was left over from it, some lingering impression of discomfort that hid in the dark corners of the Olds, breathing a tickling tongue of guilt or self-loathing or recrimination out of the darkness, making his collar feel too starchy and his ankles itchy with sweat. It was as if when he tried to picture Elaine, her rubbery black eyes and fuschia lipstick, he was prevented from contemplating that picture of familiarity, circumvented by a firm hand guiding him relentlessly back to the shock of the twenty-six-year-old losing his only son to a bullet from a .45—a bullet *you* bought, *you* loaded into *your* gun, he thought.

Jesus, I've really gotta cut this out. But he was not cutting it out, he was driving himself toward some as-yet-unseen climactic moment, the mere contemplation of which was disturbing enough. He tried to assure himself that it was long gone, he'd "dealt with it," and yet he could not deny the foolishness of so transparent an attempt at self-deception.

He swung into the driveway, surprised to have arrived home so soon. Like a drunkard in a blackout, he'd taken himself to the house as if guided by an invisible hand, caught in the steady absorption of his past, arriving with no clear sense of how he had gotten there, though he'd driven the usual route. Taking a deep breath before he hit the cold, he sighed deeply, as if in relief, then yawned hugely and convulsively. He was not expecting anything special to be happening when he walked in.

In fact, if he'd thought about it, he would merely have expected Elaine to be standing in the kitchen with a lipstick-smeared cigarette in one hand and her milk and whiskey in the other, or flipping through the afternoon paper, studiously noncommital. Instead, she sat in the big green armchair just visible in the living room from the kitchen where he entered, legs crossed sideways, hands folded in her lap, curiously immobile, and her face wore the strained imperious look of someone who is struggling to appear utterly nonchalant in the face of disaster.

"Hi," she said in a voice neither too loud nor too soft.

He peered at her. Strange how monosyllabic that word sounded in the silence that followed, as if she'd pronounced it incorrectly, condensed it into a single puff of air with the brevity befitting the seriousness of whatever situation he'd stumbled into. He froze.

"Hi." His gut rose and fell, and the dread within him, the inevitable *oh-shit* feeling, drove a slight chill up his spine. He wondered if someone in the family had died, and with the hollow casualness assumed at such moments he asked, "What's up?"

"Come on in here," she said in the same even tone, planned and orderly-sounding. This second blow to his system was a confirmation that disaster was imminent, and the effect was that of a mallet, making him relive the feeling of the little boy about to be whipped for having told a lie. He walked into the living room, sat down on the couch opposite her, and forced a smile, meant to be ingratiating, that was almost a sneer. Fear and pain had worked a fantastical contortion job on him, so much so that Elaine forgot her purpose momentarily and asked—for the hundredth time, in fact, that year—"What's wrong?"

And for the hundredth time that year, he replied, "Nothing's wrong." What could be wrong? But even he did not believe it, and he tried to figure out how to finesse the whole scene. There was nothing for it, however, except to plunge ahead with at least a modicum of honesty. "What's up with you?" he continued. "I thought something must have happened, the way you called me in here." He leaned forward, hands on his thighs.

She paused, searching carefully for words, her face a mask of expressionless concern, curiously impersonal. "Well," she began. "I want to talk to you abowt something."

"Okay."

"But I'm not sure how to start."

He softened. "Honey, you know there's naht a thing in this world you can't talk to me abowt. What is it?"

She paused again, ponderous. "Well," she said again. "I've always felt that—this is really hard for me," she interrupted herself, like an actress delivering an aside to her audience. "But...well, I've always felt that your marriage to Janice must have ended as a result of... communication prahblems."

He nodded silently, unwilling to correct her.

"Now," she was saying, "I don't feel you and I have a prahblem...communicating our feelings, that is. We've always been close."

He nodded again. "Mm-hm, mm-hm. Absolutely."

"However," and here he felt that little-kid-about-to-be-spanked feeling creeping back, "I think that lately—and I don't say it's your fault, or that it's a prahblem, only I've noticed it—there's been some kind of blockage, some sort of wall going up between us, that I haven't been able to even see before now, and—well, I know there's something wrong." She paused and studied him.

He hung fire, afraid to respond in a way she might deem inappropriate.

"And I don't know exactly what's wrong, but I feel I need to be told." Elaine said this last gently, a slight but distinct emphasis on the word "need." She continued: "I don't know if it's just me, or both of us, but I just can't help feeling that you're carrying something around with you that you don't want to carry, and it's doing something to you. It's doing something to me, too. And I don't say that to make you feel guilty or to hurt your feelings. That's naht my intent at all."

"Of course naht," he whispered hoarsely. His voice sounded strange, foreign, as if from long disuse.

"I can't let it go on, Bill. I'm willing to bear the burden of whatever this thing is, but I can't let it sit there withowt moving. Withowt *my* moving, that is. I can't stand to see you like this. I don't ask you to deny it, but I'm naht going to accuse you of something you haven't done: I just want to keep the lines of com—I take that back: I just want to *reopen* the lines of communication."

During this time she had been watching his face. He had looked alternately embarrassed, frightened, sheepish, and cunning, but most of all—and he would have been shocked at the clarity of it if he could have seen himself—he'd looked guilt-ridden. Abominably, agonizingly guilt-ridden.

He twisted his hands together, kneading them in his lap, his lips drawn tightly together like a stretched balloon. "Well," he said. "I don't know where to start."

"Start from the beginning." She had the feeling that the dialogue was out of control, as sometimes in dreams we feel someone is providing us with words not our own.

He faltered. "I mean, I don't know what to say." He was clearly struggling.

"All I want is the truth." Her voice had gone hollow, as if the spirit, or inspiration, or whatever it was, had taken over for her completely: she was on automatic pilot. Yet the feeling that he was having an affair, and that he was going to tell her about it now, was still with her, although it was receding. As if the thing that had taken her over had guided her gently into this phase of quiet and detached emptiness, she radiated a strange calm, a curious contrast to the sweating and panicky-looking man across from her who was her husband.

He told her, slowly and painstakingly, in a voice like that of a camp counselor at a campfire: a small, almost tinny voice that seemed to belong to someone else, a voice that told a horror story with the barely discernible outrage of grief rendered impotent by circumstance. He told of his and Janice's early marriage and the birth of their son, she had not known there was a child, was shocked and angered, wondering where in hell he was now, and after a cursory overview of the early married years, and of Joey's preschool bout with chicken pox, he told her about the day when at twenty-six he watched his child die in a moment of flashing light and the crack of a .45.

He held it together until he heard himself saying, "He was dead before he hit the floor. There was nothing I could do." But when the words were finally out, and all the anger and the guilt and remorse and despair had welled up in him, in tears he threw himself at her feet.

Elaine was beyond the point of being stunned, learning about the existence of Joey McCullough stunned her, but learning of his death and seeing her husband on his knees before her, Bill, who never cried, feeling his jawbone against her leg and the wetness from his tears beginning to spread through the material of her slacks...it felt like something grabbing her insides from behind her ribcage and squeezing her tight. Cast upon unbearable emotions, love and pity and anger (that he'd never told her, had borne this pointless guilt), and relief (he was faithful, always had been), and grief, she felt swept away, and she reached down inside herself for an appropriate response. She chose love, and it was as simple and natural as stretching her arms over her head in the morning, a surge of beneficent warmth that gave her the strength to confer upon him her greatest gift.

"I love you," she said. "Absolutely and unconditionally." She threw her arms around him, drawing him up to her with a single motion, and in that moment so glorious it was almost surreal, Bill McCullough began to forgive himself.

CHAPTER THIRTY-ONE

THAT NOVEMBER JEROME Brothers spent a fair amount of what little free time he had walking through the hills surrounding Carverville. Occasionally he walked through the heavily wooded areas, he felt a strange kinship with the dried-up lilac bushes and tamaracks, the huge dead oaks that still hung on somehow year after year, splendidly, magnificently decadent, and he rambled through some of the newer neighborhoods, too, gaping with unabashed surprise and horror at the plastic-looking duplexes and ranches springing up all around, vinyl-sided and with stickers still on their windows, houses that it seemed to him could never be *homes*, surrounded as they were by treeless, barren soil, by what had often been perfectly good vacant lots.

More and more, he found himself drawn to Macy's Market. He would walk up Hawthorne Street, the sun slanting down on him through murky clouds, toward the intersection where Hawthorne ran into Chestnut Avenue. Where once had been only stop signs, a traffic light now stood, like some strange yellow animal with one red, one yellow, and one green eye. Though not an unfamiliar sight to residents, still it did not seem to belong at all to the small sleepy town. "A city thing," as alien to Carverville, hanging on that slim wire and swinging in the breeze, as a spaceship or an automated teller machine. And next to it, "the Market," as locals called it.

If every person who entered the Market had had a bad word for Tom Atkins, as they assuredly did not, he would have forgiven them all. Jerome sensed this, having known the man since he was four years old. Tom had watched him grow up, so there was a sense of comfort, a wistful warmth and safety associated with the Market and, by extension, with Tom Atkins.

Jerome knew that, whether he was genial and carefree or cantankerous as an old goat, Tom would neither judge nor criticize. About the nastiest thing likely to come from Tom was, "We-ell, that's just the way it goes sometimes." And coming from Tom, at least, that was entirely sympathetic.

The store itself was a Carverville institution, the inevitable luxury of a small town: no matter who the owner was, the place had always been an exchange for new jokes and stories, local news tidbits—meaning gossip—and employment networking, which, in earlier and simpler times, had merely been called "helping." The familiar smell of creosote took on a nostalgic shade in Jerome's mind, and when he went into the Market on a Saturday afternoon in late November, the trees having lost most of their leaves, and the leaves, in turn, having nestled themselves into the hills around every house and building in town, there was a tremendous quite literal warmth that enveloped him, and a strange feeling of kinship with something ancient and unspoken that was older than him or Tom Atkins, older than the town itself. He could not have named it, but it drove a turbulence up into his chest. Leaves swirled at his feet as he closed the jangling door behind him.

Tom looked over his glasses from behind the counter. "Howdy."

"Hello," said Jerome. "Cold out there."

"Ayuh."

"How's everything going?" This was not the deceptively simple question it seemed. In fact, and both men knew this, it was pregnant with meaning: "everything" meant more than Tom and Phyllis, and in fact barely included them, it meant how was David, their ten-year-old? On an even deeper level, it was a veiled way of asking the status of the thing profoundly affecting Tom Atkins' life at this moment, a thing called acute lymphoblastic leukemia.

"All right," Tom said.

Jerome knew instantly that it was untrue. Yet, he decided not to probe. He'd heard all already: how the boy had suffered, first chemotherapy, which had ultimately borne no fruit, then some kind of radiation treatment that destroyed his immune system, prior to a massive transfusion of bone marrow (found, miraculously, when some poor trucker with a donor card had jackknifed off of route seventeen and died from multiple contusions); how they gave him Cytoxan, a type of chemotherapy that caused him violent, grueling bouts of vomiting; how he was put on a program of remission maintenance, methotrexate therapy, a regime of cyclophosphamide and something called 6MP; how the doctors were trying to build up a whole new immune system for him ("from scratch," Tom had said wryly), knowing it might not work; and how the possibilities of liver or heart failure hovered always near, keeping the middle-aged couple awake late into the night, every night, awakening them with a start early each morning.

So when he asked, "How's everything going?" and Tom said, "All right," Jerome decided that was good enough for today, and he settled into the conspiracy of silence. Nodding in response, Tom—still thinking of Jerome not as a man of twenty-eight, but as a kid, a mere child, seeing his empty sleeve where his right hand had been—seeing this, he chose to play the stoic, and it felt almost right, as if by putting the focus on someone else's misfortune for the moment, his own would be somehow a little easier to bear.

"Well," said Jerome. An awkward silence. Should he pursue the conversation in some general way, barely-disguised and trivial, feigning unconcern? Should he pursue the mundane or the bizarre? He opted for some of each, but not too much of either.

"My, uh, adjustments around the house are coming along pretty well." He shook his hand meaningfully, the way a person will when he has burned himself.

"Hah." Tom was mildly amused at the boy's bravado.

"Really. I can shave in less than twice the time it took me before, and I've even learned to sign my name." He smiled bitterly, thinking of Maria.

"Well," said Tom slowly, "you never had to do nothin' like this before."

"I fractured a wrist once, actually. It was only the left one. But still, it was pretty tough. It was either August or September, the year before third grade. Yeah, I was just a kid. I think I had just turned eight...? No, nine. Anyway, it was a drag, I remember that. Of course," he flushed a little, not wanting to sound self-pitying, "it wasn't exactly *permanent*."

Tom smiled sympathetically. "You know my son has leukemia, of course," he said, in the same way he began any conversation on the topic.

Jerome, not knowing what to say, paused for a moment. "Sure." This felt wrong, as if he should have solemnly intoned, "Yes: I know," like someone in a movie, but he blundered on anyway. "How is he? Is he making any progress, or is he in some sort of, uh, remission?"

"Well, it's tough to say. It seems like he's in kind of a 'holding pattern.' Naht really too much happening in any...meaningful way. But we have had some bad news."

Jerome felt his face fell. "What is it?"

"It's the insurance." He said it *in*surance.

"They didn't cancel you, did they?" He was ready to be outraged.

"Nope. No, they didn't cancel us. But there's a prahblem with the coverage. See, we switched from our old insurance company when he gaht sick. We could no longer afford to make the payments, and so we switched to one of those, uh, HMOs."

"Aha."

"And what they have, see, is this group of doctors, this network, and you can only choose doctors from inside that network."

"Right. It's called a Preferred Provider Organization."

"That's it!" Tom said, his eyes fiery. "A PPO. Gahd *damn* all these initials. I tell ya, it can make you crazy. Even my son's disease, they gaht to call it by a bunch of initials: A-L-L. Makes it sound like a gahddamn detergent advertisement."

Jerome said, "Hmph," and shook his head.

"Anyway, here's the thing —" he was getting excited by this, and Jerome could see that he needed to talk about it "— this damned PPO thing was a prahblem for a little while, but then we gaht it taken care of. Fownd some good doctors within the network, and took care of business, even though some of them are owt of town. But then—I'll be damned if this don't beat all—we get wind that they changed the rules on us."

"Oh, shit."

"No, no! For the better, see."

"Oh, okay."

"But wait! That's not the end of it. They changed the PPO rules, so that you can pick a doctor from owtside their network if you want to—for a little extra, of course."

"Of course."

"So now, barrin' any big prahblems, we figure we're all set. But then guess what?"

Jerome waited, silent.

"Davy gets bad, see. A turn for the worse. I'll spare ya the gory details, but the upshaht of the whole thing is this: the only doctor in the area—maybe in the state—maybe the *country*—is owtside the network."

Jerome took a deep breath. "But can't you still use someone outside the network?"

"Oh yeah! Oh yeah. But: only if he's a participating doctor—participating, here, meaning participatin' *in that HMO.*"

"And is he?"

"Oh yeah! There's just one catch." He grinned bitterly, a hideous leer.

"What's that?"

"The HMO won't cover the procedure."

Jerome was aghast. "Wait: I thought if the doctor was a participant, and you're willing to pay…." His voice trailed off.

"The basic prahblem is that the HMO has to approve treatment before the patient goes to the hahspital." His voice was toneless, and the words sounded like a prepared speech, as if he had heard it enough times to have it memorized. "Even if the doctor has approved a certain procedure, it still has to be approved by the HMO; if the HMO decides naht to cover it, the doctor is left with the option of either doing the work *for free,* or letting the patient's family shoulder the burden of payment. In a worst-case scenario, which is what we gaht here, the patient's parents might have to pay for treatment for a pre-existing condition—like leukemia—and then, since *that* breaks them, naht be able to afford to pay for another treatment by a doctor owtside the Preferred Provider Organization, assuming he, the doctor, was the only doctor around who could work that kind of magic."

Jerome sagged a little. "Can't you get another doctor? I mean, there must be someone else who can perform the operation."

"Well, if there is, we sure as hell haven't heard of him. But even so, we still can't afford it if the HMO doesn't think the treatment is *necessary.*" He spat out the word.

"There's gotta be something the people in town can do to help. Take up a collection, maybe."

"They have." Tom smiled, though he was obviously getting choked up. "They have. God bless 'em. But it's just—well, don't repeat this, 'cause I don't want folks to think I'm not grateful—but it's naht even gonna *touch* it."

"Damn," he whispered softly. "So what are you gonna do?"

"We're just gonna have to do all we can. That's all."

Jerome nodded and met his old friend's gaze directly. "All you can do is all you can do."

Tom nodded in return. "Well, I guess that's so."

They looked at each other a moment across the counter. Tom's eyes appeared almost preternatural, the eyes of a falcon or an eagle. Jerome squinted a little, as if trying to see a solution to the problem. He could not.

"Well," he said, and he hated himself for what came next, but there was nothing else to say. "You take care, now."

The thing charging the air between them, that held their gaze for those few moments, disappeared, and the shop seemed to brighten in a harsh way, sunlight breaking the clouds at a mid-March funeral.

"Thanks, thanks. You too," said Tom.

Jerome walked out, the door jangling behind him, and Tom Atkins snapped open his newspaper, sighing a long and thoughtful sigh.

When Phyllis came in, he snapped the newspaper shut again. "Hello dear."

"Hi dear." There were dark circles under her eyes, as if someone had left silver dollars on them and the coins had imprinted themselves on her flesh.

"How goes the battle?" he said.

"Well, I'm trying to keep my hopes up. I've given up praying for a miracle, but I can't accept the inevitable yet."

He looked up at her. "He may surprise us, y'know."

She resisted the temptation to shake her head. "Well, let's hope for the best," she said. Then, changing the subject: "Did you see Elaine McCullough in here the other day?"

He thought about it. "Yes. Yes, I guess I did."

"Why didn't you tell me? I haven't seen her in ages."

"Sorry. Just didn't think abowt it. But how do you know I saw her if...?" His voice trailed off.

"That's just what I was gonna tell you. I ran into her over in Oneida this morning when I went to sell m—" She gulped back the rest of the sentence.

"To sell your what?" he asked, incredulous.

She fidgeted, her eyes filling up. "Nothing, Tom, only—well, damn it, Tom, you know how things are, with David and all, and things in the store here movin' kind of slow, and the damned recession...."

"What did you sell, Phyllis?"

"I didn't sell anything, actually. I took my brooch to a pawn-broker, but —"

"Your BROOCH!" he thundered. It had been a wedding present from his parents.

"I know, dear, but it's naht something I need. Besides, I didn't sell it. That damned pawnbroker only offered me—well, I won't tell you what he offered, but it was insulting."

"Okay. Okay. Let's not talk about it anymore." He sat back and fought to control himself.

"So, how did you think Elaine seemed?"

He thought about it for a minute. He knew what she meant, but he thought about it anyway. They had known the McCulloughs for many years, almost as long as they'd known the Robbinses, knew them better, and Bill McCullough was the easiest to get to know of the whole bunch. He had an air of solicitude about him, something almost fatherly, with that baseball cap and windbreaker and those awful, funny cigars. A younger person might have called it an "aura."

Elaine was something else, a strange creature, almost pitiable. You wondered about her, hoped she was all right, thought that perhaps she'd calm down someday. You hoped. And she had not looked well, she'd seemed...preoccupied. Those rubbery black little eyes....

"She seemed a little preoccupied," he said.

"No kidding." Phyllis looked at him with a complacence that was almost contempt. "Preoccupied is right. I think their marriage is going down the tubes too."

"Wha-a-at?"

"I'm serious. She talked abowt some big, deep dark secret in Bill's past that she said she could never tell anyone. Talked as though he was havin' an affair. Or 'd had one."

"Chrissakes, Phyllis! Are you sure that's what she was gettin' at?"

"No, not exactly. But it certainly was mysterious. The poor thing."

"Hmmm. Maybe Bill is the 'poor thing' here," he murmured.

"What?"

"I say, 'Maybe Bill is the 'poor thing' here.'"

"Hmmph."

"What does that mean?"

"Well, maybe he is havin' an affair. You never know what you men are gonna do next."

"Good grief," he cried. "What's gotten into you?"

"Nothing, really. Only...I don't know. I'm just overtired, I guess. Or maybe it was that damn pawnbroker rattling my cage." There was a pause.

He sighed and searched for a change of subject. "Jerome Brothers was just in here."

She perked up. "He's such a sweet boy. How is he? Is he still dating that therapist of his? The Italian girl?"

"I don't think so. He seemed a little down, and he didn't mention it. I didn't care to bring it up, myself."

"She sounded very nice," Phyllis said. "I'd love to meet her."

He opened the paper back up. "Well, I don't know if you ever will, now."

Phyllis scowled.

CHAPTER THIRTY-TWO

LOUISE CARUSO MADE a decision one day to do something about her son's problem. She didn't know what was to be done, what *needed* to be done, only that there must be something. She had basically forgotten about having made any decision whatever, but now it was time to make another.

Things were not going well. Johnny had been increasingly brutal, in a strange, self-deprecatory way. Though bitterly sarcastic when he spoke to her, if he spoke at all, much of what he said concerned himself alone: he described himself as a lowlife, a real dirtbag, and it made her feel, of course, that somehow she was to blame. Since all the scolding and silent treatments and screaming and crying and cajoling had done no good, she decided it was time to try something else.

She would simply refuse to acknowledge it. She would pretend it never existed, and that *she* was fine. She would speak to him in cheerful, measured tones, ignoring whatever he said to her. She realized that, when he was drunk and angry, it only fanned the flame when she acted the way she did. So, if she acted as if nothing was wrong, it might anger him more, but it might make her feel better, too.

She would try it.

She sat heavily down on the living room couch with a copy of *Better Homes and Gardens*: she wanted to get out of herself for a little while. But the magazine did little good; she couldn't concentrate. She turned on the TV, and as the screen came into view, little sandwiches with arms and legs danced and sang:

Eat me, eat me,
Eat me up, now, right away.
Eat me, eat me,
If ya don't
Someone else will anyway.
I'm delicious and I'm nutritious,
So don't be silly, don't be
Superstitious,
Just eat me, oh, eat me,
Eat me up right awa-a-a-ay.

Repulsed, she hurried to shut the set back off as the announcer said, in a jocular tone, "New Peanut Butter and Marshmallow Swirl: delicious *and* nutritious. So don't be superstitious —"

She shut it off, and sat back down. Commercials were so disgusting these days. All that sex. And, although she remembered the expression "Eat me" from *Alice in Wonderland*, it still seemed like there was something vulgar about it. Johnny said something similar to her once in the heat of an argument, but she could not remember it exactly. She did not want to remember.

The phone rang.

"Hello?"

"Hi, Louise, it's Elaine McCullough."

She paused, surprised. "Hi, Elaine. How are you?"

"Pretty good, and you?"

"Very good," Louise lied. "How's Bill?"

"Oh," she said evasively, "he's okay. How's everything there?"

"Well, it's been kind of a crazy week." This was her big chance to talk to Elaine about Johnny, and she knew it. If only she could get over this discomfort, and the feeling of guilt that accompanied it.

"How do you mean?" Elaine was saying.

Courage flared up and died within her. "Well, I've had lots to do: preparing for Thanksgiving and all that." Her heart sank as she realized she was not going to tell her. Not yet at least. She was studying her nails in the light absentmindedly, noticing that there were indentations in her thumbnails, as if someone had carved part of them out. She had read somewhere this was a sign of vitamin deficiency, and felt slightly uneasy.

Odd, she kept thinking. Odd.

"Oh, I can only imagine what the holiday's going to be like *here*," Elaine said. "Bill's parents will be down from Maine, but they're both vegetarians, which is *really* strange, considering their age—-must be something to do with diet," she added, apparently unaware of the redundancy.

Louise nodded, as if Elaine could see her. "Yes. Certainly."

Elaine chattered on about the many travails of the season ("what with Christmas coming up so soon"), and Louise's attention waned again. She gazed out the window at the elm tree across the street—it had been full yellow not so long ago, she had thought of it as "her elm," and now it was barren, one tiny leaf hanging on an uppermost branch, a yellow flag waving in afternoon gloom. She sighed.

"Louise?" A pause. "Louise?"

She started. "I'm sorry, Elaine," she said, "what did you say? I was thinking about something else."

CHAPTER THIRTY-THREE

IT TOOK MARIA a long time to get in touch with Madeline Page. She got used to listening to the answering machine at the number Toni Myers gave her: "Hi. This is Madeline Page. I'm not here now, but please leave your name, number, and a brief message, and I'll get back to you just as soon as I can. Wait for the beep…."

Each time, Maria left only her name and number, but Madeline Page had not contacted her, and the messages were getting more and more terse: "Maria Santisia. My number's five-seven-three…"

Finally, on a Friday evening at about 8:30, Madeline Page called. She'd been trying to get ahold of Maria for days, she said. Was she a friend of Toni's?

Yes, Toni had given her the number.

They agreed to meet the following Monday at 7:15 at Madeline's house, since Maria's work schedule conflicted with regular office hours.

In retrospect, Maria remembered what happened during and after the appointment only vaguely: Madeline Page was pleasant; Madeline Page recommended intensive counseling, much to Maria's dismay; they strongly disagreed; finally, upon learning that Maria had an employee assistance program, Madeline Page recommended a "brief vacation" at a place she referred to casually and cryptically as a "Codependency Treatment Center." It would most likely be covered by insurance, she said, under "Psychotherapy."

At this, Maria's brow contracted: psychotherapy was not part of the plan.

Then came a series of phone calls to obtain more information on the center. Madeline Page did not know the details, had only learned of the program through a friend of a friend. But her rich, throaty voice sounded immensely reassuring, and so Maria began the process of calling stranger after stranger.

"Hi, my name is Maria. I got your number from Madeline Page, and she thought you might have some information...?"

It was like trying to track down someone from the CIA, she thought, but eventually she got the number. She hadn't wanted to make any of these calls, and above all, she didn't want to go to this place. But she had been assured that the place was not a "psych ward," and felt almost impelled to action by some force outside herself. She made the necessary arrangements.

Arriving, she anticipated paper slippers, detached probing questions: "Any history of mental illness in your family? Have you ever visited a psychologist or psychiatrist?"

Instead, a youngish, slender woman with brown hair and warm, wide-set green eyes welcomed her and asked her to fill out some paperwork. The preliminary information was nothing more than basic background, like an unusually spare job application. Only toward the end of the form were there any questions pertaining to her stay: Did she have any health problems? Any mental health problems? (Apparently so, she thought with a wince.) What did she think the problem was? How would she define her personal relationships?

She was introduced to other members of the group—other patients, she thought—on a strict first name basis: Maria. Brian. Stephanie. It was all casual, almost pleasant, and only became more business-like when the small, green-eyed woman returned and gave them each a prepared list of the center's rules and regulations. There was to be no smoking anywhere in the building; no contact with people from the outside; no sexual relations between guests; and no "isolating." A set schedule of daily events had to be followed with measured exactitude, though there were some unscheduled afternoon and evening hours each week.

Maria felt a little trapped, particularly by the "no contacts" rule, but she had little time to brood on this. The green-eyed woman, whose name was Jean, handed everyone a huge packet of mimeographed articles, their titles somewhat arresting, even mysterious. *What is Abuse? How Do Adults Feel? Roadblocks to Communication. Setting Boundaries. Love or Obsession?* This one sounded especially soap-operatic to Maria.

"I don't want you to feel you have to read all of these, either during the week or after you leave," Jean told them. "You're free to do what you choose with them, although they all come highly recommended." She smiled her enigmatic smile before she went on. "But for now, we'll put them aside and talk about why we're here. Or specifically, why you're all here."

She talked about her own background briefly first, apparently to reassure all newcomers that her credentials were solid, then talked about abuse of various types: gender abuse, sexual abuse, spiritual and emotional, physical and mental. She explained that in her view, all people were, without exception, victims of abuse, particularly of themselves.

She insisted on the primacy of "stuffing" feelings in our culture, a concept the group appeared to understand. Jean described the self-imposed "censor" who tells the potential parricide or rebellious housewife that his or her very thoughts are impermissible, outrageous, or shameful; the moral arbiter of the Self, operating under the clever guise of conscience, but whose purpose is to inflict guilt, fear, and self-hatred, whose ultimate goal is attained when honesty becomes impossible, and the barriers of common indifference and uncommunicativeness are firmly in place and apparently unshakeable.

She spoke with quiet eloquence, and Maria was impressed. Only half believing what she heard, she felt nonetheless that it could be true. And frightening though that possibility seemed, it was also possible that something good could come from acknowledging it.

And then the therapist talked about codependence.

"You've all heard the word *codependence* or *codependency* before: in some pop psychology book, or, if nothing else, in the name of this center."

They all tittered, some with manifest nervousness.

"Well," she went on, "the question remains: what *is* it? Now, I guess that, on a basic level, we're all codependents. I mean, we're all affected by other people's behavior to *some* extent, and that's basically what we're talking about here—not necessarily dependence. The problem of codependence arises when someone is out-of-control —" she strung the words together as if they were one, her head swaying exaggeratedly on her neck like a whooping crane "— and I mean *out-of-control*. A raving codependent. And I don't mean that insultingly, because I *am* one. Let me explain.

"Probably you had a grandmother or great aunt or somebody who was a raving codependent. The Ultimate Caretaker. You know the type? Takes care of everyone but herself, compulsive worrier, complains about the "million-and-one" things she *has to do*, loses sleep over other people's problems while trying, unsuccessfully, I might add, to make everyone happy, and making herself miserable in the process." She held a fist to her chest when she said *herself*.

"Or how about your father, or grandfather, or uncle? The stoic. Let's say it's your brother. Every time you mention some difficulty to him, he feels a need to 'fix it.' No sooner do words come out of your mouth than he's presenting you with options A, B, and C."

The group chuckled uneasily again.

"He is constantly advising, and proposing solutions, and analyzing and diagnosing and scrutinizing, and *probing* for personal information, examining and dissecting and espousing and expounding and prognosticating—you get the idea." Laughter, nods of agreement. "In short, manipulating. Trying to shut you up, or off, because he doesn't like the way *you* discussing *your* problem makes *him* feel. And understandably so. Does any of this sound familiar?"

Nods, chuckles, and sounds of assent from around the room.

"Well, okay, then," she wound up with a flourish, "you're in the right place!" The group laughed, offered smatters of applause.

"Now, the question is probably still running through your minds: 'Why am *I* here, then? Why not all those other people?' I can't answer that one for ya. I could say *they're* the crazy ones—certainly not *you* lovely people." She again smiled that enigmatic smile, as the group tittered again.

"And I could say that I need help just as much as all of you—which is true, by the way. Or I could just take Thoreau's advice: 'Simplify, simplify, simplify.' Which is probably the best course of all. So let's do that. Since we're here, and not Uncle Clem and Aunt Martha, I'm going to do what I can to help you, and all I'm going to ask for is cooperation and open-mindedness—the latter of which is far more important, believe it or not. Fair enough?"

More nods and murmurs in the affirmative.

"And one thing, please." She smiled broadly. "No threatening gestures toward me or other staff members. Or others in your group. No fingerpointing, yelling, or clenched fists. You'll find that most of our group sessions here are very relaxed and informal, and it'll be a lot easier for you to be informal if you're relaxed. You're not going to be raked over the coals or 'confronted' by me or anyone else. More than anything, you're here to get in touch with why you're here. I don't know if that makes sense to anyone, but I hope it will by the time you leave. So, let's have some lunch! I'm hungry."

With the biggest smile yet, Jean led them into the cafeteria next door.

Altogether the week was strange and disturbing. For once, Maria was more or less forced to look at and think about herself only, and not focus on anyone else. Some assignments dealt with other people—one of which was to write a letter to each of her parents in which she discussed childhood feelings—but even this was ultimately oriented toward thinking about herself, and helping resolve inner conflicts.

She and the other guests were also asked to write letters to people with whom they'd had difficulties, and one of hers ended up being a long, rambling, emotional letter to Jerome. In it, she poured out long-suppressed feelings, mostly rage. It surprised her, even frightened her a bit, to see how bitterly angry she was.

Above all, she learned she had a right to her feelings, anger included, and that it was possible to work through whatever came up. She had a right to be frightened, to be sad, to be happy. They were just feelings. But they were *her* feelings, and it was okay, she was told, to own them. This brought relief, since she had always been slightly ashamed of her feelings.

One difficulty of the experience concerned her energy level: she had grown accustomed to walking a full seven miles a day, and had tremendous energy as a result. In the program, she did not have time to do that. At best she had about half an hour before a meal during which she could walk two miles or so. But she had a terrific urge to expend the excess, and did it by throwing herself headlong into group activities.

One of her favorites was experiential therapy, where group members acted out the roles of other members' relatives, in what often turned into surreal, tear-drenched miniplays. There were films to watch, handouts to read. New friendships were made and strengthened each day as more commonalities came to the surface, conversations lasting until the inevitable "lights out" at eleven o'clock.

Most importantly, she learned about what one therapist called "setting boundaries," which meant deciding what behavior she would, or would not, accept, and asking for, or even demanding, what she wanted and needed from the people in her life. And as she opened up to this concept—as much a revelation, in its way, as her anger—the voice in her head that had been saying over and over *I don't want to be a codependent* began to be replaced by a quieter, stronger voice that simply said *It's okay to be here.*

By the end of the week, Maria looked at herself in a way that demonstrated a new reflectiveness. The staff asked her and the rest of the group to assess themselves in terms of areas of difficulty, of their emotional, mental, and spiritual growth, and of where improvements could be made. Everyone pledged to attend a certain number of meetings per week of an appropriate support group, leaving each other on friendly terms.

They exchanged phone numbers, and laughter and good fellowship ended the day, but when she left, she felt tired and vulnerable. In a way, she felt stripped of her flesh, but she knew she would grow a new skin, and soon. And she knew that this skin would feel better, in spite of fears, in spite of pain and of the emotional rollercoaster, and that it would fit better.

PART THREE

"Ah, surely nothing dies but something mourns."

— LORD BYRON

CHAPTER THIRTY-FOUR

THE MCCULLOUGHS DID not go to the Robbinses to play setback until the day after Christmas. Elaine looked buttoned up, her fat blue coat wrapped around her like a dark sausage skin and closed at the neck, her head, swathed in a scarf, jutting from the coat with all the impudence of a frog bobbing up for a fly.

Bill glanced at her little black eyes and garish lipstick as he escorted her toward the Robbinses' door, sighing a bit: she was a good woman. Neither of them, after all, were what they once had been, but they were on intimate terms, at least, since he'd told her about the death of his son.

He lifted the heavy brass doorknocker and let it fall with a clank, Elaine at his side. He thought for a moment of the many times in the past when she'd asked him what was wrong, how they had accumulated, how she had stoically accepted his "Nothings." He felt a little sorry for her, and admired her, too; she seemed brave and strong. He was happy.

Ed opened the door, looking rumpled. "Hi ya," he waved, "come on in."

Bill thought of the perfectos and white wine of their last card game and smiled. "Merry Christmas, Ed."

Ed Merry Christmased and Happy New Yeared them into the living room. Bill looked around, assessing the place with cool discomfort. It seemed a long time since they'd been there, and the atmosphere was different now. It was strange, as if the thorough, ritualistic cleaning the house had just received put a strain on it—the walls hanging back, ready to burst, and many of the knickknacks, and even the furniture, appearing restored from some mysterious state of decrepitude. A fake, nauseating smell filled the air, almost antiseptic, and Bill noted it—that goddamn lemony shit they polish the furniture with—as he and Elaine sat down.

The new closeness between Bill and Elaine was obvious. They sat opposite each other, quietly, like lovers in a restaurant. Ed and Margaret sat at the far ends of the small kitchen table—Bill and Elaine approximating intimacy, Ed and Margaret an insurmountable distance. They had not been to counseling.

While Ed shuffled the newly-opened deck, Bill said, "What a prahblem we had this week at the shop."

"Oh yeah?" Margaret yawned behind her hand.

"I'll say. Someone had ordered a bunch of business stationery and envelopes, see. I don't remember for sure, but I think they were Greystone five-and-a-halfs —"

"Waitaminit," Elaine interrupted. "They're naht gonna know what 'Greystone five-and-a-halfs' are, hon." She waved a finger back and forth between Ed and Margaret.

"Well," said Bill, "I've been in the printing business for so many years, I forget this stuff isn't common knowledge. Anyway, okay, Greystone five-and-a-halfs are envelopes—regular envelopes, mind you, not windows."

"Greystone is the name of the company that makes 'em?" asked Ed.

"No, no, it's just a color name, like 'ivory'…or —"

"Teal?" Margaret offered.

"Exactly. They're just these grey envelopes and stationery, but the company couldn't just call them 'grey.'"

"What else d'ya have?" asked Ed.

"Well, you got your basic papers—Vintage Bahnd and Vintage Linen—and those are abowt the same quality, both have abowt a twenty-five percent rag content —"

"You lost me. What are you talking abowt, 'rag content?'" asked Margaret.

"Well, okay—a brief lesson in papermaking: when I say 'rag content' I'm talking abowt cotton content, which is usually arownd twenty-five percent." His hand cut the air for emphasis. "At least for Vintage Bahnd or linen."

"Those are brand names?" asked Margaret.

Ed shuffled the cards.

"Right. See, back in the old days—thowsands of years ago— they used cotton in papermaking. A few hundred years ago, in Europe, they'd developed papermaking to a pretty fine art, and were using rags and all kinds of stuff to make paper. We're talking good paper, the kind you don't see anymore. Eventually, that became too expensive, so cotton came back. Most of what you and I think of when we say 'paper' has some cotton in it. We do have vellum, though, which is strictly sulfite."

"Which is...?"

"Wood chip, as opposed to cotton fiber. See, when paper is made, it goes through rollers, which press it tighter and tighter. It's called calendaring. Now, if you have twenty-pownd bond paper in both hands, and you feed one pile between rollers that are set for normal and the other between rollers that are calendared heavily, or pressed heavily, then the second one will come owt thinner. Understand? Vellum isn't calendared, so it's not embossed, but it has a smooth finish."

Ed smirked. "I think you lost me." He dealt everyone their cards.

"Well," Bill said patiently, "normal business papers are sulfites, okay? So they're wood chip, not cotton fiber. Anyway, the whole point here is this guy had ordered a large quantity of these Greystone five-and-a-halfs, which are a vellum-type paper, a sulfite, as opposed to cotton. In other words, the good stuff."

"Yeah?"

"They never came in. Now, he needed the stuff in an hour. And ultimately, it didn't matter what type of envelopes or paper he got. He just wanted something quality, like for résumés. So there he is, waiting patiently, while we're in the back trying to crank owt these five hundred Greystone five-and-a-halfs, except that they're not Greystones, they're Vintage Linen, which is inferior by comparison. And every once in a while I've gotta come owt and tell the poor guy 'Sorry 'bowt this, but we'll have some stuff ready for ya in just a couple minutes.'"

Margaret perused the hand she'd been dealt. "Does that sort of thing happen much?"

"Oh, no, not all that much. In fact, our suppliers generally get us everything we need. It's just that something...I don't know, van broke down, something. We still haven't fownd owt."

Ed looked over the hand he had dealt himself, appeared bored. "I'll bet that guy was pretty upset."

Bill slouched back. He seemed to think about it for a moment. "Not really," he said. "He was very understanding, actually. People usually are, if you give 'em a good deal, and explain the circumstances." He looked down at his hand.

"Well," said Ed, "I don't know abowt that."

The conversation lagged as each player looked at the cards. For the rest of the night there was little talk other than game-related banter. Bill noticed that Margaret seemed strangely distant—she had not kissed him hello this time, and was curiously silent most of the night—but he chalked it up to her letting Ed perform. And perform he did, the ultimate host in grand style, laughing and joking, pouring drinks with dogged persistence.

And throughout it all, Elaine continued to glance at her husband, trying to catch Bill unawares, but to no avail. More than anything else, she was smiling, a bit sheepishly, acknowledging the fact that Bill's "affair" with Margaret had all been in her head. She wanted to reassure him that she was reassured.

The evening came and went. Ed grew louder and sillier as the night progressed, only this time it was especially noticeable. Bill felt himself and Elaine grow eerily quiet, and Margaret virtually invisible, while Ed seemed to be forcing himself to entertain, as if he were under terrific stress, trying to prevent his own internal combustion. His face the color of a boiled crab, he laughed hoarsely, tears coming to his eyes.

"Well," Elaine said at last, "I think we'd better go."

"Aw, come on, you guys!" cried Ed. "Less have another drink. Me and Bill will have one, right, Bill? *You* can drive, Elaine, heh heh heh."

Bill rose, looking serious. "Really, Ed, we'd better be going."

Ed picked up the stern tone. "Well, okay." Then, exaggeratedly jovial, "But you two be careful on the way home now. Don't get caught in any *snowdrifts*! Haw haw."

"Good night, Margaret," they said ponderously, their smiles strained like masks.

"'Night," she mumbled. She hugged them half-heartedly.

"Good night, Ed." Smiles of condescension, shaking of hands.

"G'night, folks," he bellowed. "And don't get caught in any *snow*drifts. Haw haw haw!"

CHAPTER THIRTY-FIVE

TOM ATKINS SAT quietly in his store. A late January afternoon, the sky lowered itself down over the land, became a greyish mass of implacable clouds. He looked out the window, watching the traffic light swinging in the wind. His hands hung limply between his knees. He was too tired to feel like going to war with himself. Phyllis came in softly.

He looked up. "How is he?"

"He's resting," she said, skirting the issue. She came over, stood behind him, put her fingertips on his right shoulder, and whispered, "I don't think he's going to make it, Tom." Her fingers clenched his shoulderblade.

"He'll make it. He'll make it," he repeated, but he heard his own lack of conviction.

"No." It was scarcely a whisper. "It's that damned bone marrow," she said. "They said it was a match, a one-in-a-billion miracle. But they were wrong." She paused before raising her voice. "Remember when he took a turn for the worse? Back before Christmas, when we had to have that young intern work on him?"

"Sure, I remember," he said bitterly. "If it hadn'ta been for the goddamn *in*surance, we wouldn'ta needed no intern. I remember."

"That's what we're faced with now. He's taken a turn for the worse again. Only this time, I think it's the one thing we were all most afraid of."

He waited, and when she did not continue, he said, "Host-versus-graft." She did not respond, but he knew, he could tell by the cessation of pressure on his shoulders. "The new marrow is attacking his organs." It was almost a question.

"I think so," she said, tears in her voice.

"What about that drug they're s'posed to give him for that?" he cried suddenly. "Cyclosporin, or whatever the hell it's called. Doesn't that *do* anything?"

"I don't know," she whispered. "I don't know."

He sighed, sad and empty, sank into the silence. "Jerome Brothers came in this morning," he said abruptly.

This was something he'd only begun doing recently, changing the subject when he got uncomfortable. Phyllis noticed the pattern, but decided that to comment on it would be a breach of faith, and she'd gone along with him.

"And how's Jerome Brothers today?" There was no denying the note of irritation in her voice, but she merely sniffled quietly and wiped tears away with the back of her hand.

"I dunno. It's funny, but every time he talks to me abowt that therapist of his, Maria, I can't help thinkin' he's going to try to get back together with her, and *I* don't know what to tell him. Hell, I don't know if it's a good idea or naht, but I don't wanna advise him against it. Seems to me if she were really interested, she'd have come arownd by now. They had a big blowout, but that was quite a while back—months ago." He studied his hands.

She moved back and away from him. "I don't know as I'd give him any advice, unless he asks for it. My father always said, 'Phyl, if there's one thing in life you gaht to learn, it's when to keep your mouth shut.' Most folks don't ever learn, 'cause they're always mindin' someone else's business other than their own. I'm not saying you're doin' that with Jerry Brothers, but it wouldn't be too hard for me to fall into it… I avoid it like the plague. I just nahd my head and say. 'Oh, that's too bad,' or whatever, but I don't hand owt pronouncements if I can help it."

"I know what you mean. Still, it'd be nice to have some input, I think. I can't help feelin' that's what the boy's lookin' for, though he's too polite to hint arownd."

"Well," she said dubiously, "he doesn't exactly need our approval."

"I know. Just seems like he wants some encouragement."

"Listen. If he talks to you about her again, my advice would be to tell him that, if she calls, he should play it cool, but not discourage her. Maybe even suggest that they get together. If he's plannin' to call her, though, he better be prepared to have a phone slammed down in his ear, 'cause if they haven't talked in that long, there's probably a good reason. You say they haven't talked in *months?*"

"I don't think so."

"Well, good Lord, Tom, that girl could be married by now."

A faint smile played about his lips. "I kinda dowt if she's gotten married, dear."

"You know what I mean, though. A laht can happen in a couple months."

"Right."

"Besides," she said, and her facial muscles tensed for just a fraction of a second, "we got enough troubles of our own without worryin' about Jerome Brothers' domestic affairs."

He looked at he floor, silent. "I know," he said, and after that they did not speak for a long time.

CHAPTER THIRTY-SIX

A TERRIBLE INERTIA gripped him as he stared at the phone. He'd planned to call Maria Tuesday evening but managed to put it off, resolving to call Wednesday instead. Now it was Thursday. He'd worked all day, he was tired—but that was not excuse enough to put it off another day. Besides, he thought, nobody's home on Friday nights.

He allowed himself some ambivalence. Hadn't his last words to her been, "You can bill me for the writing lessons—*and for your other services?*" He winced. Maybe it would be better to just forget it. He might not ever see her again. He might not even want to, really.

But he could not escape the responsibility, and he knew that if he at least called, at least made the effort—even if she wasn't home—he could say he had tried. He dialed.

Strange sounds echoed on the other end of the line. He heard a ring, then a click, and the sound of a song playing, which came in over the sound of the ringing phone. Surprised, he pulled the phone away from his ear, but he heard only the sound of dead air as the ringing abruptly halted and Maria's quiet alto came over the line.

"Hello?"

He caught his breath.

"Hello?" she repeated.

"Maria, this is Jerome Brothers." He heard the sharply indrawn breath, and paused an instant unintentionally.

"How are you?" she asked, neutral.

"Okay. Listen, please don't hang up. I have something I need to say to you."

He heard a slight sigh, as of impatience. "Okaaay..."

"Look. I—I know I was very nasty to you, the last time we were together." He paused, but she did not disagree. "I want to apologize for what I said. I've wanted to call you for a long while, but I thought that—well, to tell you the God's honest truth, I was...afraid to call. I didn't know what you'd say, and I still don't know what you're going to say, but I don't want to leave things the way they were. And I understand if you don't accept the apology, but—I needed to make it." He paused again, relieved that the confession had tumbled out.

"I thought you didn't believe in God."

He was suddenly off-guard. "What?"

"You said *the God's honest truth*. And I said *I thought you didn't believe in God*." Her tone was absolutely neutral.

"Listen, that's—that's part of my apology, too. I mean, I apologize for that. You're entitled to your beliefs, and it was wrong of me to be blatantly disrespectful of them." He was going to continue, but she interjected:

"Well, it's definitely not a good idea, for someone who wants to be friends with someone else, to *not* respect them or their beliefs. It makes the idea of friendship kind of an oxymoron."

"Well, it made me look like an abso*lute* moron," he said.

She laughed, in spite of herself it seemed. "Listen, I didn't intend to ram spirituality down your throat," she said, and her voice lost some of its cool neutrality. "Maybe I was partially to blame for what happened. But, anyway, neither of us chose to call the other, and that's all water under the bridge anyway, at this point. I mean, I think that what offended me was you seemed to think that, um, just because you didn't get what you were praying for, that therefore there couldn't be a God...as if God were some sort of cosmic bellhop: a *Magical Genie* whose job was to grant your every wish."

He chuckled self-consciously. "I must've sounded pretty arrogant. I'd never really thought about it much. God, that is. I s'pose there could be a God —"

She laughed. "Oh, that's nice and generous of you —"

"— and, uh, yeah, it is, isn't it?" He chuckled again. "Hoo boy. Anyway...I don't know, I just, uh—I was a strange kid, you know?"

"I'll bet."

"I really was. And I never really had a religion or anything like that, because in our house it just didn't exist. It wasn't an issue. I know we went to church a couple times, but only a couple that I can recall. But anyway, any belief I might have had just got totally wiped out, I think, when I was in college. Mostly as a result of my, ah, shall we say 'hedonistic pursuits?'"

"Mm-*hm*."

"I guess I developed a real cynicism about life in general, and I was very bored, and restless, and confused when I graduated. I had no passion left, none whatsoever. I was spent."

"That's sad."

"I guess it is. And you know, I had this feeling that I was going to settle. I mean, that I was gonna end up getting married just out of fear of being alone. And I fought that, I really did, and I've worked at staying out of those kinds of relationships. But all along, deep down, I've had this feeling that after all of these little tentative touches in theaters and after all the other little foolish fencing matches I'd find myself in, I was still going to 'settle.' Inevitably, eventually, most definitely, I would settle. Not just settle down. Settle for second best, or worse."

"That's scary."

"Yeah. So when I met you, I thought, 'Wow. Now her, *she's* not settling.' And, I'll admit it, I pretty much thought of you as someone I could only aspire to be with."

"Flatterer."

"No, I'm serious. I realize that the nature of the whole thing has changed, and that's okay. I'm not low enough to try playing on your emotions, to think you'd succumb to flattery."

She hesitated. "Well, good."

"I just want you to know the truth. I feel bad about screwing things up, but, hey: I can't change the past. Can we at least be on speaking terms in the future?"

"Of course," she said. "In fact, I was thinking—I've been working a lot of hours, and I haven't been doing too much on the weekends. Would you want to maybe get together this weekend if the weather's okay?"

"Sure, how about dinner?" He cringed at how eager he sounded.

"No, no. Just for coffee or something. Just to talk." There was a smile in her voice.

"All right," he said. "How about a walk in the park? Maybe on Sunday...?"

"That sounds almost too corny. Can I bring a friend?"

"I'll tell you what," he said. "I'll bring two friends, if I can: Ed and Margaret Robbins. You haven't met them, I don't think."

"No. They're a married couple?"

"Yeah, and they're a few years older than us, but I think you'll like them. I haven't talked to them in quite a while, actually, and this would sort of kill two birds with one stone, if you'll pardon the expression."

Maria laughed. "That is an awfully barbaric expression."

"Yeah." He smiled. "It figures, doesn't it?"

She did not answer, but merely said, "Why don't you give me a call tomorrow around six, and I'll let you know, okay?"

"Great. I'll talk to the Robbinses later tonight."

When they had both hung up, he sat back on the couch and heaved a sigh of relief. He touched his fingers to his forehead, found it damp with perspiration. Thank God, he said to himself. Thank God.

CHAPTER THIRTY-SEVEN

ON THE NIGHT of his birthday, January twenty-eighth, Johnny Caruso obtained a gram of ice, that peculiarly potent form of methamphetamine that had become his friend, wife, lover, and travelling partner. Like crack, the drug was smokable, and Johnny fashioned himself a sort of pipe out of a beer can and some aluminum foil with pinholes punched in it. Smoking by himself, he hunkered down in the front seat of the Camaro, eyes bugging, behind an abandoned apartment building on Harper Avenue. It hit him like a bomb, this savage incredible rush, and he fought panic down with a slug of peppermint schnapps.

Jesus, this shit's unbelievable.

He breathed out the last hit through his nostrils, dragonlike as he settled into a dreamy buzz. He'd blasted off, he was on some wild amusement park ride that lifted him into an ethereal no-man's-land, and he hung there, floating down like a leaf on a windless day. The schnapps tingled in the back of his throat, mentholy, as minutes ticked away, and he was safely out of the "danger zone" of near blackout, his heart pounded in the cage of his chest, he could feel it thudding, and rage welled up, it seemed to grow, surging upward in direct proportion to the loss of his initial high, as if the closer he got to earth on his downward float, the more potent the rage became, until at last he was livid, his teeth gritted and jaws beginning to ache badly, he heard a distant gurgling and rumbling deep in his bowels, and rage mounted to his throat. "Fuck," he said aloud. "Fuck. Fu-u-u-uck."

He started the engine and drove mechanically out of the lot muttering to himself. He could hear his voice, "I'll fuckin' kill her," but it seemed to come from somewhere else, a disembodied voice, too low and strangely plaintive to be his. He drove toward the home of Sandra Andrews, the leatherjacketed brunette who had disapproved so loudly when he'd slipped LSD into Jerome Brothers' orange juice. Something in him was beginning to snap, he was not sure what it was, but the rage was mounting to the backs of his eyes, and he shook his head defiantly before it could overwhelm him. He felt like, if he let it, it would thrust him through the windshield of his car.

Rounding the corner, he began the slow ascent up Wells Drive to Sandra's house, aware only now of the difficulty of driving and that he was compelled toward Sandra for reasons he could not understand. Before long, he was stumbling out of the Camaro, lurching against it, nearly breaking the schnapps bottle in the process, breathing a sigh of relief upon realizing it was intact, and, uncapping it, taking a swig from it.

Whew. Unb'lievable.

He regained his bearings, so it was not necessary to lurch up the stairs. In fact, he was able to walk almost coolly, swaggering up to the door in a manner that felt amazingly ordinary. He banged on the door with one clenched fist, resisting the temptation to shout out her name.

"Johnny!" Her eyes looked huge, and her tousled hair was swept up and moussed into a stiff, soft-looking arrangement. She wore a short white skirt with pleats.

"Lemme in, I gotta talk." He swayed slightly.

"Nobody's home," she answered, but apparently that meant she had carte blanche, since she swung the door open. "You're *wasted.*"

"Yeah," he smiled. He looked proud, except in the eyes, which did not smile, but retained a hint of fierceness, and contempt. She would never forget those eyes.

"So what are you doin' here?"

"Let's go for a ride," he said, ignoring the question. He slouched into the kitchen, and leaned against the refrigerator: wary, immobile, hands in the side pockets of his coat.

"I really can't go anywhere, Johnny. Sorry. My dad's expecting a really important call, and I need to be here t— "

"Screw your dad," he snarled. "Let's bail." I'm gonna hurt her, he thought.

"Johnny," she said, looking stung. "That's not very nice. Hey, you wanna smoke a joint? I can't leave, but we can —"

"No," he interrupted, "I don't wanna smoke a joint. Do I fucking look like I need a joint?" I'm gonna nail her.

"Okay, man, screw you. I don't care."

"There's an idea," he said, and with the force of an explosion he was upon her.

"HEY," was all she had time to say, and then his body rammed against her like a huge fist, she could smell peppermint schnapps hard in her face as they collapsed on the floor, and she cried out as he wrestled her across the kitchen, tumbling into the living room. She banged her head against the leg of the couch and bright light flashed in her eyes, she cried out one last time feebly before he stuffed the tail of a shirt that had been lying on the floor into her mouth, he tore at her clothes, the viselike fingers prying her legs open as she smelled the stale tobacco smell of his hand on her mouth. In a moment, fighting would be useless, and suddenly (Oh God, oh God) the moment was gone, and the terrible tearing sensation seemed to rend her in two, it went on for what seemed longer than it possibly could have, and she choked back hot tears, the taste of the shirt coppery and rancid in her throat: involuntarily she'd begun to swallow it, and she choked on it, gagging, before he was finished. He left her there, crumpled on the floor with her skirt up, as he staggered out the door, breathing hard into the night, she was gasping and sobbing uncontrollably as she heard the sound of the open door squeaking in the wind, a harsh icecold draft sweeping over her, making each part of the wounded flesh sting with magnified force, she rocked back and forth on the floor, feeling the goose pimples hardening on her legs, and the only thought she had was Goose pimples. Goose pimples.

CHAPTER THIRTY-EIGHT

ON THE FIRST Sunday in February, Carverville was reaping the dubious benefit of a delayed "January thaw," meaning a rise in temperature from a median of twenty-three degrees to a whopping thirty-four. Jerome was grateful for the small change in weather, which made possible the walk in Bruford Park with Maria and the Robbinses. They'd all agreed to meet by the statue of Nathaniel Hawthorne that gazed stonily down on the gnarled tamaracks and maples, the benches and paved parking lots.

The statue had an interesting history. It seemed unlikely that Hawthorne had ever even visited Carverville—then a borough of Johnson City—and no one knew its significance. Most people in the town assumed that Hawthorne was born there, or had been the mayor, at least. In fact, the statue had been erected at the request of Carverville's second mayor, Edmund Viscount, who had migrated from Paterson, New Jersey, in 1899. An avid Hawthorne reader, Viscount had been partly responsible for the formation of a borough in Passaic county north of Paterson called Hawthorne. At the turn of the century, Viscount travelled by way of the Susquehanna railroad to Johnson City, New York. The city was in need of glass and hosiery, which Viscount managed to provide through a shrewd and complicated business deal with the founder of a large local shoe industry, which would eventually become Morrow's through a merger.

Ultimately, Viscount founded Carverville in honor of his personal hero, John Carver, the first governor of Massachusetts' Plymouth Colony. Carver had been credited with negotiating a particularly effective treaty with local Indians in the early 1620s. The statue of Hawthorne was a whim Viscount could afford to have satisfied, even over the murmured objections of locals who wanted a statue of Johnson City's George Johnson to be commissioned. Viscount's fondness for Nathaniel Hawthorne, and his personal involvement in the formation of Hawthorne, New Jersey, combined to influence his playing this exquisite—he thought— practical joke. Had he lived to see that no one in present-day Carverville knew the statue's tortuous history, he would have roared.

When they met in front of Viscount's Hawthorne on this cold February afternoon, Jerome and Maria were impatient to talk, although a peculiar reticence made their conversation sound much like that of old friends newly reunited, slightly awkward and constrained.

"Hi," he said on seeing her approach.

They both smiled.

"Hello," she said. "How's it going?"

"I'm okay. Cold." He shivered.

"Me too. Seems like I never get used to it. Lived here my whole life, too." She smiled more openly.

His heart lifted. "I know what you mean." He paused. "You want to walk?" he asked.

"Sure. Where we going?"

"Not far." He glanced at her. "We're meeting them here, so we'll have to pretty much walk in circles— stay within view of that statue," he said, pointing. "But at least we'll be warm."

"Mm-hm."

Their heels clicked on the pavement. He did not smile again, but only said, "You look well."

"Thanks. You too. I'm feeling okay: I went away for a while, not long ago—" She hesitated for a moment.

"Where'd you go?"

"We-ell, it's kind of a long story."

"We got time." He checked his watch, frowning ironically like his old self for a moment.

"Well." She walked faster. "Remember when we had our little—altercation?"

"Mm-hm." He winced.

"After that day, I started going on a lot of long walks. Extremely long walks. And I was doing it every day, rain or shine."

"Hmm."

"I was getting to the point where I could identify cars by the smell of their exhaust. You know: needs a catalytic converter, running on leaded gas."

Jerome laughed.

"Hey, Brothers!" came a voice from the other side of the green. It was Ed. "What's that pretty lady doin' with *you*? Ha ha ha!"

Margaret swatted him on the arm with her gloved hand. Maria laughed silently.

"Yeah, that's them all right," Jerome said drily, and smiled. The conversation lapsed as they walked toward the statue.

"Hey, old sport!" said Jerome. "How are ya?" They made introductions.

"Jerome's told me so much about you," said Maria.

"Oh, us too," Ed mumbled. He looked abashed.

They moved off as a group, aware now that it was too cold to stand around.

"Did you know Jerome's aunt and uncle?" asked Maria.

"Oh, yeah," Ed said. "Even before they moved to the Adirondacks. I think Margie and me always regretted that we never gaht to say goodbye to 'em." He paused, significantly and solemnly. "They died owt there, you know."

"Oh," she said, unsure of what to say. She opted for silence.

"Yeah, they left me the house even before they moved," Jerome said. "My uncle was getting on in years. He didn't want to try to keep up the yard and all that, although that was always one of his first loves."

Maria looked at him, surprised. "Really? I don't know too many people who like yardwork." She smiled.

"Well, my uncle was one of those people who was very close to the land, always. He knew all the plants and wildflowers around here—"

"Wow."

"And he used to point them out to me on these little 'nature walks.' In fact—get this—the main reason he moved with my aunt to Port Henry was because of a bog."

"A *bog?*"

"Uh huh. He was fascinated by that sort of thing. Kind of like spelunking. They discovered this glacier-type thing, it was called a 'glacial kettlehole,' and it was bordered by a rare acidic bog. I want to say 'arboreal,' but I don't think that's the right word: I think it was acidic."

Maria smiled. "Gee, I hate to sound ignorant, but what the heck is a glacial kettlehole?"

"Well, during the ice age there were huge glaciers, see. Now, let's say you've got a big chunk of ice—thirty, forty tons—"

"That *is* huge...."

"Right. And it sits there melting, year after year. Well, the water erodes the ground, but the ground absorbs it, so you get a kind of crater. Which eventually fills up with water. That's a kettle pond."

"You're making this up," Maria smiled.

"No, I'm serious. My uncle was fascinated with that bog, see. It sustained all kinds of plants: winged monkeyflower, kidneyleaf mud plantain, orchids, sundews, pitcher plants...all kinds of strange things."

"Kidneyleaf mud—?"

"Plantain. That's an endangered plant. It's against the law to even pick one."

Maria smiled at the Robbinses. "Can you believe him?"

"Fascinating, ain't it? He's a reg'lar encyclopedia, our Jerome," Ed said. He pursed his lips in a parody of a smile, his face skull-like in the merciless February sunlight.

"Sorry, Ed," Jerome said earnestly. "I know how that stuff can get boring in a hurry. Say, speaking of plants —"

"Uh oh," Maria said.

"— here's a story for ya. Well, actually, it's about leaves. You know those trucks they use to collect leaves from in front of people's yards?"

"Hmm. Not sure."

"They're big yellow trucks. Leaf-shredder trucks, I guess you'd call them. Anyway, I was driving down the road one day, a couple months ago, and I got behind one of these things. I'm going along about twenty-five miles an hour, and I can see this little opening in the back of the truck with all these shredded leaves packed in. And they're flying out onto my windshield: little tiny flakes of dried leaves, like a snowstorm. It was the weirdest thing. I mean, it wasn't like it created hazardous conditions or anything, it was just bizarre. Kind of…eerie, you know, but peaceful?" He shook his head. "Anyway, I don't know what made me think of that, but for some reason I remembered it just now."

"Kidneyleaf mud plantain?" Maria said, and they all laughed.

"That's what did it," said Jerome.

They all fell silent for several moments, as if no one knew what to say.

Across the park three crows flew up from the ground into a maple tree's uppermost branches. *Auk*, one called out. *Auk, auk.*

"So," Maria said, and came to a halt. "Look at those crows. They look like ravens or something, they're so huge." She pointed at them.

The four of them stopped to look.

"Yeah," said Ed. "There's Heckle and Jeckle. But who's the third one: Freckle? Haw haw haw!"

Margaret rolled her eyes, while Maria giggled. Jerome merely grinned. Good old Ed. It was tough to take things too seriously with him around.

They walked on, and Maria fielded questions about her job. She countered Ed's thinly-disguised hints about her relationship with Jerome, saying, "I'm not seeing anyone now."

Eventually, they made several revolutions around the park, and although they were warmed from the exercise, as the sun spread out in the western sky, a breeze came up to chill them. It was nearly four o'clock when Ed and Margaret said goodbye, exclaiming to Maria that it was a pleasure to meet her, and admonishing Jerome for being "such a stranger." Then they were gone.

"I never knew you'd gone to school in California," Jerome said. "I was really surprised when you mentioned that to Ed earlier."

"You never asked," she said. "Why were you surprised?"

"I don't know. At first I thought it was because I can't picture you in California, but that isn't entirely true. I think I was just pleased to learn something I didn't know."

She smiled. "There are lots of things you don't know about me. And vice-versa, no doubt," she added quickly.

"What else don't I know?" He gave her a grin.

"Well, let's see. Did you know I have a B.S. in occupational therapy?"

"No, but I'm not surprised. That's a B.S. in 'O.T.' then, eh?"

"Right," she said. "I'm also affiliated with the American *and* the New York Occupational Therapy Associations —"

"Ooh," he said, and smiled devilishly.

"What else?" She paused. "Did you know that, originally, you were supposed to come to the med center for your therapy?"

He stopped abruptly. "How come I didn't have to?"

She grinned. "I arranged that."

"Wha-a-at?"

"'The usual procedure is for the patient to receive OT for a period not less than three days,'" she recited, "'but not more than seven without express written consent of the HMO —'"

He jabbed at her side with one finger, tickling her, and she began to laugh.

"You were so sneaky," he said, as she squirmed.

"Stooop." She laughed harder.

"You set it up."

"Wait a minute!"

"I'll fix you," he said, and got her just beneath the ribs before she escaped with a little scream. They stood there, laughing, panting, until they were ready to continue walking. It took a moment for his heart to slow. "So, what else don't I know about?"

"Well," she said gravely, "remember back when I told you I'd had a dangerous liaison with someone who was married?"

"Yeah?"

"What I neglected to mention was that I was married at the time too."

"I see...." He put his chin in his hand.

"I know that sounds sick, but I'm not a criminal. It was a loveless marriage: a youthful mistake, I guess you could say."

"I see."

"You keep saying that. Like you're about to give me a traffic ticket or something."

"I'm not a cop," he said, smiling.

"I know that."

"I'm not a lawyer or a judge, either. Or a marriage counselor. I'm just kind of surprised you were married in the first place."

"Why? Why wouldn't I be married?"

"It's not that, it's just that—I don't know, I can picture you in California, but I can't picture you in matrimony at all. How's that?"

"You're silly."

"Hey, I can't picture *me* married. I mean, it's nothing personal, it's just—surprising, that's all."

"Anyway, I thought you should know. It kind of felt like unfinished business, you know what I mean?"

"I know what you mean," he said. "I felt like there was unfinished business between us until I called you and apologized for what I said."

"I'm not apologizing for being married, you understand —"

"Oh, of course —"

"—just for neglecting to mention it. That was almost like lying, looking back on it. Sort of a 'sin of omission.'"

He smiled. "I don't know if I'd go *that* far."

"I would. But it's all water under the bridge at this point, right?"

"Water under the bridge," he said. "Hey, I just thought of something else: how did you set up coming to my house in the first place to give me that therapy? Wasn't I at least supposed to go back to the center periodically, as an outpatient? That was the impression I got."

Her eyes sparkled. "I was responsible for that. I said there were extenuating circumstances, and they let me do it my way, since I requested it."

"Oh," he said quietly. "Okay." And he smiled to himself as they walked on in the falling dark.

CHAPTER THIRTY-NINE

IT DID NOT begin dramatically, with a heart attack or kidney failure, just a rash on his arms and legs that could have been anything, but was more: the rash was little David Atkins' first visible symptom of host-versus-graft disease.

Tom and Phyllis sat like statues in the waiting room, day after day, while the doctors struggled together, trying to beat back the inevitable. Only at certain times were the couple allowed into the room to see him.

On February fourth, after a failed attempt to get his white cell count back to a manageable level, a team of nurses and doctors watched in tearful frustration as David succumbed.

They were prepared, they thought, for their son's death. But neither could have predicted what they felt when Doctor Evan emerged from the green room, his eyes red and glistening above the surgical mask. When they saw his eyes they knew, and in that moment, they clung to each other like a couple stranded in a blizzard. The hot tears flowed.

Tom would never forget the sensation of floodgates opening, when his head filled with countless swirling thoughts. His heart was empty. At the bottom of his emptiness lay a great anger, and as he began to recover strength, anger mounted in his chest like something tangible, ignited by just one question: why?

Phyllis had some of the same experience, but her anger felt more like a balloon being blown up, and when it had been filled to a certain point, there was a sudden deflation into sadness. And something else happened to her, something which she could not explain or understand, but which she shared with him anyway on the day after the funeral. They'd asked to be left alone, and the visiting friends and relatives respectfully granted them some solitude. Phyllis got beside her husband and knelt on the small space of floor next to his chair with his hand pressed between her own smaller hands.

"It was strange," she said. "I was feeling like my heart had been torn owt of me. It's such a difficult thing, between a mother and child, you know that; it was a big deal to *you*—the father-and-son thing, I mean…."

He nodded sadly.

"Anyway—I was sitting there in the bedroom, looking at all his things and feeling sadness like nothing I've ever felt. And just when I didn't think I could bear another second, I heard this voice in my head—well, it wasn't a *voice*, more like I'd had a thought in the midst of it all that was very strong and clear. And it just said, 'All is well.' And that surprised me, because I didn't believe it, and I sure as hell didn't *feel* it, but the next thought I had was, 'Love one another.'" A chill seized her spine, and she gazed at him there, her heart overflowing. "All those years, sleepwalking through life—but now I know every moment we had together was a miracle."

"Oh, God, Phyl." He threw himself into her arms, pressing himself to her shoulder, and began to cry, very hard and almost as if in relief.

CHAPTER FORTY

AT TEN O'CLOCK on a Saturday morning, Bill McCullough's phone rang. People rarely called before noon on weekends, so he expected it to be one of Elaine's relatives. He was taken aback when he answered and heard a familiar voice:

"Hey, Bill, how'sa boy?"

The gritty voice had jolted him. "Ed...?"

"Sure, it's me, all right. How's everything goin'?"

"Good, good. Are you all right?"

"Oh, hangin' in there," said Ed. "Listen, I gaht a question for ya..."

"Yeah?"

"Do you know anything about lathes?"

He paused, thinking. He'd been in printing so long, it seemed like some other lifetime that he'd worked with metals or wood.

"Naht really, Ed," he said. "It's been a while since I did any work with that kind of machinery."

"Hmmm..."

"In fact, the technology they have now prahbably makes what I know obsolete!" He laughed shortly, a muffled sound.

"Jeez," said Ed. "That poses kind of a prahblem."

"Why, what's up?"

"Well," he said, "I've got this lathe here at home, see —"

"Uh-huh."

"— And it's gaht a lowsy taper on it."

"A lowsy *taper*?"

"Right. A taper. It's located on the tailstahck. Now, what I need, see, is a three-degree Morris taper. It's the only self-holding, self-releasing taper there is, as far as I know. The rest are miserable, see, and that's what I've gaht."

Bill's patience was wearing. "So, Ed," he went on, a forced smile in his voice. "How can *I* help with this?"

"Well," Ed said and paused as an audible *psst* came over the line, the sound of a can being opened. "I was hoping you might have a lathe, or know someone who has one I can use."

Bill pressed the phone closer to his ear. "Hey, are you *okay*, Ed?"

"Sure, never better. Why?" There was the sound of a long slurp.

"I dunno," said Bill, "just seems funny hearing you ask about lathe work. I mean, you being in the carpet business 'n all. Nothing personal, though, pal, just concern."

"Well, thanks pardner, but I'm A-OK. Just doin' a little side-work is all." At this, something in his stomach rebelled, but he fought it down, as if Bill could see him through the phone: he could not betray this discomfort.

"Sorry I can't help you owt," Bill was saying. "Fact, I don't think I even know anyone who owns a lathe, other than yourself."

"Ah, well, that's all right. So how's Elaine? Everything okay with you two?"

"Sure, sure," he said. "Fine." Look who's asking, he thought in spite of himself. "Yeah, Elaine's over at her mother's place today. Something abowt fruit baskets or something, I forget." He laughed, a bit self-consciously. Dear Lord.

"Good, good," Ed said, as if he were listening.

"How's Margaret?"

"Oh, pretty good, I guess," he said. "She's working time-and-a-half today." He ran his fingertips around the golden can of Miller, tapping the letters that seemed to blare out from the side of the can, as if announcing themselves. There was a tremendous tremor within him, a kind of vibration that manifested itself in his fingers when he tried to move them separately, or hold a piece of paper steady. He was okay if he kept moving or kept perfectly still.

Bill began to talk about the Super Bowl, how great it had been, how much he was looking forward to baseball season now that spring was nearly here. He was talking about various teams, the Dodgers, the Mets, the Red Sox, others, too, but Ed could no longer give him his undivided attention. He could hear other sounds in the room, other voices, as if two or three people were carrying on a muffled conversation on the other side of the wall. With rising panic, he realized he had not turned the TV on, and, just as suddenly as they began, the voices ceased, and Bill's reassuring baritone continued uninterrupted, droning cheerfully on about batting statistics and some pitcher's ERA.

"Listen, Bill?"

He halted abruptly in mid-sentence: "Huh?"

"I, uh—I gahtta go."

"Oh. Okay, Ed. Take it easy, huh?"

"Yeah. Yeah. You too," he said hurriedly.

"See ya round town."

"Okey-doke. Bye."

"Adios." *Click.*

Ed drained a last gulp from the can, hoping it would quell the trembling he still felt within, if not without, and Bill McCullough looked dreamily out his window, imagining the approach of spring.

CHAPTER FORTY-ONE

PHYLLIS ATKINS' HUSBAND was not speaking with her.

It was not because she had done anything; indeed, she had to atone for neither a sin of omission nor commission. It was something much deeper to battle, a vast insidious gulf that had opened up between them, a rift irreparable and invincible, something he created by his silence.

He was not speaking. He did not know what to say.

She would come into the store and find him standing at the counter, gazing blankly ahead, gazing out the window at nothing at all, seeing nothing and almost being nothing, all his energy concentrated into the clenched fists he held before him like twin hams. And she, feeling more helpless than angry, stood there behind him, waiting (for him to turn around? for him to say something? she did not know herself), waiting on and on until, at last, she succumbed to the wifely instinct that made her question him:

"Are you all right, dear?"

He would nod, or perhaps merely turn and smile wanly—it was not a smile, truly, could not have been called a smile: that tremor around the lips, a shadow of a smile, like a flicker from some pale neon light that has sputtered out, but holds a last spark within it. Sometimes he only nodded once, a barely perceptible inclination of the head or shoulders—just enough to indicate he'd heard, felt her presence, although she could scarcely have known this.

And he knew that a chasm had opened between them, he, too, felt it: it was as if he were suffocating still in the messy gauze wrap of their grief, and she had escaped it somehow, and there she stood, unfettered, breathing in the roseate air of a new day while he waited in helpless, immobile, astonished fury. And he knew he seemed somehow impotent to her, if not literally then figuratively, he seemed drier, tighter, to himself. He even looked a little shrunken in the mirror, he thought, studying the circles beneath his eyes.

He could only talk about the effect on his work, his operation of the Market—things had gotten backed up, there were orders to fill and refill, things to be done, and he would occasionally refer to the days before David's death, obliquely, as "before all this": exemplifying, with one poignant hand in the air, the emptiness and despair and anger and guilt and frustration and even his estrangement from her with the authority and economy of movement of a consummate actor. But an eloquent gesture was not enough, and she felt obliged to try to penetrate his anger, help him nurse it if necessary, examine, nurture, and own it, and even perhaps to work it out, as it were, yes, work it out, to help him feel what he needed to feel and get beyond it, she thought. It was eating him alive, anyone could see that.

And he just sat there, his head either in a whirlwind or mercifully blank. The whirlwind spun with the names of drugs David had had to take, Cytoxan, Cyclosporin, and the names of other things that had been important—doctors' names, favorite comic book characters, TV shows, toys. When his mind went blank, it felt like there was nothing alive on earth but himself, Tom Atkins, and this grief holding him, numb, in its grip.

Phyllis walked into the store, gazing along the wall at familiar displays of homemade jellies, the stovepipe and canned goods, wrenches, boxes of Fatima. Tom moved slowly among the cigarettes behind the counter, loading up the little blue and red and green and white packages with a leisurely air that could have indicated either indolence or sadness. She knew which it was.

"Morning, dear."

He looked bleakly up, smiling politely at her: a formality. "Morning."

"How ya feeling?" she asked, coming around to his side of the counter: a little woman, still attractive to him, although her hair was quite grey now.

"I'm okay," he said. "You?"

"Oh, can't complain." She smiled at him, almost reproachfully, in the mute language that must inevitably pass between two who have been together so long. "Need a hand there?"

"No," he said. "Thanks." He continued to stock the cigarettes in the plastic-encased rows above him. It occurred to her that, with his hands above him, his chest straining against his shirt as he moved, he looked as though he could have been something other than an entrepreneur. An electrician, maybe, or a carpenter.

"Well," she said. "Nice day, for a change. First one in a long while."

He looked out the window at the sunny mid-March morning. "Yep."

There was a long pause. She thought about whether or not she should go on, saddened, and a little angered, even, that they had been reduced to small talk. He continued to stock the cigarettes.

At length, she said, "Tom."

"Yeah?" The response was merely obligatory. He did not stop his stocking.

She nearly said, "Never mind," but did not. While she deliberated—suddenly at a loss—he said, "What?"

"You really loved him, didn't you?"

For a moment, he was not sure he had understood. "I what?"

She gathered herself up, taking a deep breath, letting it back out. "You really loved him, *didn't* you?"

"Of course I loved him. Why are we talking abowt this again?" His eyes flashed, although his tone had remained neutral.

Again she braced herself. "Because," she said, "this is either something we're going to have to get through together, or it's going to *kill* one of us." She stared at him. "Or both," she added.

He looked down. "What are you saying, Phyllis?"

And again she braced herself. "I'm saying I want you to talk to me." She moved closer, searching his face.

He glanced up at her. "What do you want me talk abowt? What am I supposed to say?"

She stepped toward him, took the cigarettes out of his hand, and led him away from the counter toward the tall window. "Just talk to me," she said. "Just talk."

And he did.

CHAPTER FORTY-TWO

THE FIRST DAY of spring dawned bright and cool, and Jerome and Maria were together again. They had not seen each other since Bruford Park with the Robbinses, but he'd called twice to say hello. She had not called—she wanted to be friends, she said, but was taking time to "work on" herself. He asked for no details. But she agreed to meet when he suggested it.

So now they were together again, except that this time they met at Jerome's house and went for a drive in his old Ford. He had suggested a walk, but she was trying to cut down, she said. They headed west on route seventeen, near the state college, trying to tune in the oldies station on the AM radio.

"I don't think I'm going to get it in any better than this," she said, making a final attempt to subdue the crackle of static.

"No problem," he said, dismissing the radio with a gesture.

"What if it were?"

"A problem? Well, you know what they used to say in the old country, right?"

She smiled. "No, what did they used to say in the old country?"

"*Tough shit!*" He laughed maniacally, and she shook her head at him, laughing softly to herself.

"Excuse my French," he said at length.

"That *wasn't* French."

"I know, I know."

"French would be 'merde,' I think."

He laughed again. "You know, they say the curses of the future are going to be related to *different* taboos: not sex anymore, or bodily functions, but things like death, or money."

"For example?"

"Well, you remember Duncan Scrump?"

"Yeah?"

"Well, since he was a multi-billionaire, it's been suggested that blue-collar workers might use his name as a curse."

"Like what? 'Scrump you?'"

He laughed. "Yeah, or I'm really scrumped off."

"What about death?"

"Sure, people have had euphemisms about death for ages. It's inevitable that, as people loosen up about sex, and even the old homosexual epithets become unacceptable, we're bound to get increasingly more squeamish about death. Especially with all the emphasis on Youth and the Youth Culture, and the proliferation of senior citizens in America. It's just inevitable."

"You're a regular prophet. So what's gonna happen? You're saying you think people will start talking about corpsing around or something?"

"I dunno. Maybe they'll start using more of those old 'I hope you rot in Hell'-type things. Or, let's see, how about, 'Hey, if you even wanna *live* to see a hundred and ten....'"

She laughed. "Plus we'll have all these people getting old, and fighting it every step of the way, of course."

"God, what a hideous spectacle."

"Hey, I thought you didn't believe in God."

He glanced over at her, and she smiled mischievously. He seemed to relax, settling down into the seat. "Sorry," he said. "I guess I shouldn't use the word that way."

The sincerity surprised her. "Oh, I don't mind," she said, then paused. "But God might."

They laughed.

After a long silence, he said, "You know, we have some really weird conversations."

"That's okay. Any other type of conversation is usually boring to *me*."

"I've always thought of 'ordinary' as being synonymous with 'boring' too."

"It's not just that," she said. "I usually have pretty mundane conversations with my patients: small talk, talk about their therapy—beyond that, my circle has been pretty limited lately, so the conversation I've had hasn't been all that interesting."

"I know what you mean. Nothing but 'work' and 'the weather' for me." He rolled his eyes.

She patted his shoulder and gave it a friendly squeeze. "I want you to know I really enjoy your friendship. I mean, I value you as a friend."

He glanced over, dividing his attention evenly between her and the road. "Well, thanks. I mean, seriously, I joke around a lot, and I may have made you uncomfortable with references to the past, but I feel the same. And if all we are from here on in is friends," he said decisively, "then that's okay."

He slapped his leg lightly for emphasis, but did not believe himself. And there was a long pause during which he was aware only that she seemed to be smiling contentedly. He felt an actual warmth in the car.

After the glow of the moment had passed, she asked, "How are Ed and Margaret Robbins?"

His eyebrows went up. "Funny you should ask. I just bumped into Margaret Thursday."

"Really?"

"Yeah, at the supermarket. She seemed to be doing fine, but she didn't have much to say about Ed. I even asked her."

"What did she say?"

He pondered it. "I think all she said was, 'Oh, about the same.' I don't think she was being nasty or sarcastic or anything, but the way she said it was weird. Almost like he had a dis*ease* or something."

"Maybe he does," she said slowly.

"Huh?"

She appeared to consider. "I get a funny feeling about Ed. Like there's something not quite right about him."

"That doesn't mean he's sick, does it?"

"Not necessarily. But there might be something wrong there. And her saying, 'About the same' in that way kind of supports that. Does that make sense?"

He tapped the steering wheel lightly. "Yeah," he said, "it does. It makes a lot of sense."

CHAPTER FORTY-THREE

JOHNNY CARUSO WAS speeding through Carverville. It was Saturday night in April, nearly three months after the rape, and he was desperate. Sandra remained silent, yet he had fantasies of silencing her now. Choked by remorse, he'd skipped school, avoided her at all costs, getting only angrier in the process. Now he zoomed down Chestnut Avenue, taking hits off of a crack pipe while telling himself pointedly that he was cracking up.

The pun was intentional. He'd mixed his new love, the powerful amphetamine *ice*, with what remained of a small stash of crack he'd been doling out to himself. The process was common, and the mixture had been nicknamed "crackup." Only the tempering influence of peppermint schnapps kept him from driving off the road altogether, and, as it was, he occasionally hit the button for one of the power windows and leveled a loaded pistol he'd bought for a hundred dollars at a passing speed-limit sign. A thirty-eight Smith and Wesson with a handle grip, it weighed about as much as a small hammer.

There was no telling what would happen next. He knew that. Gone were the possible refuges of Dweeper, Ronnie Mazursky, or the rest of the group. He'd alienated himself from each of them systematically, either by dismissing them as unimportant, or through some overt act of intimidation. By now, they were all disassociated from him. Even the younger girls turned away now, bored, frightened, or worse still, indifferent.

He shifted gears, wheeling into the dark sanctuary of Bruford Park.

Well, I told my friends goodbye...

He slowed down and shot out a street light. The report echoed in the dark, a lonesome sound. Glass tinkled on the blacktop.

And I rode down to the station...

He shifted again, pushing her up toward fifty as he reached the top of the hill.

And I never said goodbye...

The lights of the little town lay beneath him like stars.

When I left this failing nation...

At the crest of the hill, he decided to coast and found himself braking in his slow descent toward the stop sign at the bottom of the hill. The schnapps was almost gone, but he took another small mouthful, budgeting it in case he needed more later. He eased the power windows down part way and pulled over beyond the stop sign. A little stream of cool air rushed in over him, making his nostrils dilate slightly and the flesh on the back of his neck bristle. The hell with budgeting: he finished the schnapps.

What the fuck good was it, anyway? Who really cared? And, more importantly, would anyone in the world understand? It seemed unlikely. Peasants, he thought. He spat out the window. Slaves.

He held the gun in his left hand, mesmerized by its dull weight on his palm. It was powerful, he felt that. It *was* power: the power to kill, the power to give and take, to confer or remove. Power. He moved it slowly out the window and aimed at the throbbing blank of darkness.

"Bang," he whispered. He jerked the hand back slightly in imitation of pulling the trigger. "Bang."

There was no answer. Only the distant sound of peepers, whose strident *weep-weep* kept the wind from being the lone sound in the park.

"Bang," he whispered again. He pulled his arm back into the car, set the gun on the seat beside him, and began to move off.

Someone would surely report having heard the shot when he took out the streetlight. And in this town, he thought, the cops'll be here in about five minutes. Give 'em a break from the donuts, anyway.

He pulled out onto Fairbanks Drive and tried to keep to the speed limit for "safety's sake." No need to get pulled over for driving under the influence. He hoped Louise would be asleep by the time he got home, and when he finally arrived, he tiptoed into the house, carefully turning each doorknob, swinging the doors quickly and almost noiselessly in turn.

When he entered his bedroom, he locked the door before even turning on the light, making sure that Louise couldn't confront him, in case one of the small sounds he'd made upon entering, or the sound of the Camaro in the drive, woke her. He clicked on the lamp, a small bulb wrapped in dark red plastic, so that the light was almost blood-colored. It was his one concession to "atmosphere," the single romantic aberration in the room, but in his present state, it struck him only as ghastly. He didn't look at himself in the mirror intentionally, but he caught a glimpse of his disheveled figure in passing and was almost amused. In a brief moment of clarity, he saw the insanity of being almost amused at his own corruption, and the thought made fear leap up in the pit of his belly, gurgling like a growl of hunger.

"I'm cracking up," he whispered aloud. He chuckled.

He lay on the bed in the red light, listening to the silence outside his window. He was slowly coming down from the crackup, but only at a torturous rate. In the near-darkness, he saw the silhouette of his face on the wall and heard the thudding of his heart in its cage. It sounded in his ears like the booming of cannons in a faraway valley.

CHAPTER FORTY-FOUR

ED ROBBINS WAS not going for counseling.

Margaret found her initial triumph to be a hollow victory, and had tried cajoling, demanding, ignoring, and even imploring, all to no avail. He had apparently agreed to go to counseling in a moment of madness, and obstinately refused to consider the option of "talking to some nitwit headshrinker" now.

To compound the problem, his drinking seemed to have picked up, though she'd cut off his allowance after a particularly nasty argument. Presumably, people at the local taverns took pity on "poor Ed, whose wife is a real bitch-on-wheels," as Margaret put it to herself. She had had enough.

She'd planned her separation carefully and secretively. She met with the attorney and arranged to get a legal separation, set up a tiny one-room efficiency on which she'd paid a deposit with money she'd squirrelled away, skipped or skimped on lunch for longer than she cared to remember, and worked overtime often to pull off the secret security deposit. But in the end, it was relatively easy: Ed was still too cowed by her new role as breadwinner and by his own joblessness to question their finances.

In spite of all this, she agonized over how to break the news. She loved him still, hoped against hope, and wanted him to see the situation and make some changes—changes that might change her mind. She felt curiously ambivalent, but at certain moments, which she considered her worst, she thought the announcement should be a joyous affair: a declaration of her freedom to his face, or, more appropriately, *in* it.

At other moments, she pictured herself delivering a quiet and steady lecture "on the importance of communication in a relationship," which would end with a clear, almost kind explanation of why she could not go on with him. It would be more like a mother/son talk than a husband and wife talk. Somewhere in the middle of these two extremes lay the more balanced version she secretly hoped to find, but she doubted her capacity to strike a balance, her anger and guilt throwing her so off-kilter.

That was a curious thing, too: why *guilt?* She had done nothing wrong, so far as she could see. In fact, she'd worked harder than ever at taking care of him since his layoff. What did she have to feel guilty about? And yet that nagging voice chided her whenever she was raging, *Couldn't you be doing something more? Couldn't you try a little harder? Are you being fair about this?*

Having resolved to tell him in whatever way necessary, she finally gathered her courage. It was a Saturday afternoon, she had just been notified that her new apartment was ready for occupancy, and a strange now-or-never urgency pushed at her.

Ed, gone since breakfast on some minor errand, surely sat somewhere having a couple. That strengthened her resolve. She decided that, no matter how long she had to wait, she would tell him that day. Her heart pounded while she contemplated the scene, but she kept busy, to stave off the effect if possible, by simply employing the principle of motion.

She cleaned, straightened, dusted, and ironed until the effects of keeping busy wore off. But then she found herself getting angrier and angrier, watching the hours slip by: three o'clock; four o'clock. Five. She prepared dinner for both of them, although she was sure he would eat none of it, and in spite of the rage building up in her, she felt concern, too. What if he'd been hurt, had an accident somewhere? What if he was already at the hospital, and they just hadn't called yet? The phone could ring any minute.

When he slouched in at six-thirty, she was sitting in her favorite chair, nursing a bad case of indigestion and pretending to read a paperback. Half-filled pots and pans sat on the kitchen stove, still warm, but beginning to smell stale.

"Hi, honey," he said. He walked into the living room, moving toward her with a careful but steady tread.

She did not answer.

He stopped before he was within ten feet of the chair. "Hi," he repeated.

She still did not reply, only closed the book and looked at him from beneath veiled eyes as if he were some relatively interesting, if harmless, reptile. "I'm leaving you," she said, her voice level and without emotion. But her heart fluttered.

"Huh?" His mouth hung open. "Whaddya mean?"

He appeared to want to go on, but she would not allow it. "I'm leaving you, I said. *Today.*"

"Chrissakes, Margie, ya can't leave!" he groaned. "I need ya here, babe. I'm sorry abowt dinner, but I ran into Pete Rosario, and you know how long-winded Pete is...." Desperation filled his voice, although he tried to appear casual.

"Goodbye, Ed," she said, rising. "You'll be hearing from my lawyer." Her heart pounded. "I'm sending you papers."

"Margie, for God's sake," he cried, following her to the bedroom. "You can't *do* this!"

"I am doing it," she said. It was not a time to argue, she knew: in a moment, his pleading would turn to rage.

"Margie," he said. "Margie, don't do this. You're not really gonna *do* this?" He leaned against the doorjamb.

"Watch me."

"Jesus Christ!" he cried.

Here it comes, she thought.

"I'm right at the point where my wife most needs help around the house, and—and where I need her most, and she just fucking bails out. Leaves me stranded!"

"Nice language, Ed." She pulled the packed suitcase from the bed.

"Oh! Oh!" he brayed, like someone greatly wronged, wounded. "That's right. Little Miss Priss. Drag owt all the old shit." He grimaced in imitation of her, bobbing his head back and forth like a young boy: "I don't like his *clothes*. I don't like his *jahb*. He *swears* too much!"

"Ed."

"What?" he snapped.

"Ed, I said you'll be hearing from my lawyer. I'm sorry it had to be this way —"

"Oh, *you're* sorry! Ha! What a good one *that* is."

The smell of scotch drifted by, making her stomach clench. She bit her lip: arguing back was futile. "Goodbye, Ed," she said quietly, dragging the suitcase out into the hall.

"Yeah? Go ahead, leave! You'll be back," he said, following her.

"Goodbye," she repeated. Her heart still pounded away in her chest.

"And naht only that," he went on, his voice rising, "you'll come back with yer tail between yer legs. Unnerstand?"

She did not speak, but merely set down the suitcase, opened the front door for herself, and heaved it out while she propped the door open.

"You'll regret this," he said, "lawyer or no lawyer. And I don't care *what* kind of a Jew lawyer you get —"

"Adios," she interrupted, and with that, she was gone.

He continued to rave from the front parch, but she was already tuned out. Occasionally she caught a word, but overall the sound was incoherent: bitch...house...all my life...lawyer. It did not matter.

She only knew that, as she began the ascent of the driveway, swinging the big wagon at last onto the quiet pavement of
Sycamore Road, she began to calm down. Her pulse did not slow
immediately, but in her excitement, she felt something different,
she did not know what. And then she realized she did not recognize it because she had not had the sensation in such a long time:
she was elated.

She turned on the radio, tapping her fingers on the steering
wheel as she approached the stop sign at Sycamore and Mill, she
checked herself briefly in the rearview mirror and saw that her eyes
were clear as noon, turned up the radio, mashing down on the gas
when she pulled away from the stop sign, and throwing her head
back in laughter, she laughed and laughed, and she did not stop
until she was only a few hundred yards away from her brand-new
efficiency apartment.

CHAPTER FORTY-FIVE

EVERY NOW AND then, Bill McCullough dug into one of his many mythology books as a diversion. It was an odd habit, he realized, because it was not exactly research, but it was not light reading, either: more a purposeful skimming. He allowed himself this occasional eccentricity only because it was so infrequent a lapse, and because he was otherwise "a regular guy."

This time, he did not find what he was looking for, although he found some fairly grim tragedies. There was a story about someone who abandoned his son in a cave, and another about a son who killed his mother to avenge his father. Nowhere was there a story about the anguish of a father who feels responsibility for his son's accidental death, although there was a story about a father who had killed his son: Tantalus, son of Zeus, who had boiled his son Pelops and tried to serve him up, like a roast of mutton, to the gods. The gods saw through this shabby stunt, and set up a special hell for Tantalus, a pool in Hades where he could never satisfy his monstrous appetite or insatiable thirst. He would be forever *tantalized.*

It was far removed from his situation, of course—Bill had hardly murdered his son—but the punishment seemed familiar, the endless agony. His agony was at least coming slowly to an end.

Finally, he came across something that made him think, another story that mentioned a son: Achilles, champion of the Greeks, son of Peleus and of the sea nymph Thetis. When Achilles was born, Bill read, Thetis, hoping to make her son invulnerable, had dipped him in the River Styx. But she had not been careful enough to cover the part of his heel by which she held him, that vulnerable part of skin and tendon that would come to be known as the Achilles. When Prince Paris, son of Troy's King Priam, shot Achilles there with a poisoned arrow, he died, for that was his one vulnerable, mortal part.

The lesson Bill gained was that there was no magic River Styx, no solution into which he and his first wife could have dipped little Joey, no foolproof protective wrapping to shield him from the big, dangerous world. A car might just as easily have hit him. As it was, he had been alive on this planet, had died on this planet, had blown his brain out as unwittingly as someone who steps on a banana peel. Now, sixteen years later, Bill began to see that. That was just the way it was sometimes.

He sighed, closing the book and closing his eyes. He was all right for now.

"In the depth of your hopes and desires lies your silent knowledge of the beyond;
And like seeds dreaming beneath the snow your heart dreams of spring."

— KAHLIL GIBRAN

CHAPTER FORTY-SIX

JEROME BROTHERS WAS walking in the woods near Bruford Park. It was the last walk he would take alone that spring, and in his odd way he savored that aspect of it. Maria had taken him there, parked her car, and gone running—she had replaced walking with running, she said, reasoning that it took less time and was just about as beneficial. She would meet him by the Nathaniel Hawthorne statue in an hour.

He checked his watch, saw that he had forty-five minutes before he had to meet her, then wandered down into the thickly wooded area bordering the industrial park that lay on the outskirts of nearby Endicott. A trail had been blazed there, probably by the Civilian Conservation Corps or somebody, back before he was born. They'd marked it with spots of yellow paint on trees, apparently in no special pattern, and the marks were frequent enough that he could follow the labyrinthine trail without thinking too much about it, as long as he took his eyes off the ground from time to time.

He passed a man, and that was strange: not the fact of seeing someone, but because the man was so unnaturally well-dressed. A businessman-type, most likely in his thirties, he wore a three-piece suit. What was he doing in the woods in a three-piece suit? Was he lost? Had he murdered someone out there?

He mumbled a quick "How y' doin'?" at Jerome, and Jerome nodded, smiling grimly. The look in the man's eyes troubled him, but he could not place it. He walked on, lost in thought, and when he looked back over his shoulder, the man was no longer in sight.

Then it struck him: the slightly smug look in the businessman's eyes, a look he'd seen in the eyes of many men, usually in their thirties or forties, it seemed, belonged to someone with a good job, a wife and children, maybe, two cars in the garage; someone too old to be afraid of everything, yet old enough to be afraid of his own mortality; someone who realized that, although he looked like he had it all together, he was angry inside, frustrated, frightened; someone who felt his life slipping away from beneath him, while he clung desperately to the well-trimmed lawn, the respect of his colleagues; someone who could not help sensing the sharp stench of his own corruption, even as he tried to turn his face away.

Jerome shuddered.

He ambled down to the stream and gazed down on it contentedly. Too early in the season for insects, but everything was coming into bloom. Green moss, tinged by patches of yellow and brown, lay like a soft carpet along part of the water's edge, and a tree leaned over its own reflection.

He walked along, hand in pocket, and eventually discovered something strange on the water: a toy boat, stuck against a floating branch which, half submerged, had stalled the small toy's progress. He poked at it with a stick, loosening it from the branch, but it caught on another. Freeing it again, he watched it sail away, stately, like a barge floating unmanned down a wide river. It floated out of sight.

Time passed slowly, but it was well spent, and when he met Maria at the statue, he felt contented and calm. She told him about a strange dream she'd had the night before about Moravian folk heroes called the Klishnas, half-human and half-kangaroo, and he laughed, because he had crazy dreams too. They walked a little, then returned to the car.

"Let's go to my place," she said.

And they spent the night together that night, although they slept in her bed as if they were only old friends, comfortable and without the pressure of romance. It was not until the morning, when he heard her voice waking him up, that the thought of love-making became possible.

"Good morning."

The spring sun filtered down through a crevice between the window frame and shade, warming the room. Maria was snuggled down beside him in the bed, her breath drifting across the back of his neck.

"Hi." He stretched, arms over his head. "Be right back," he said, giving her shoulder a little squeeze. "I'm just going to jump in the shower, okay?"

She did not open her eyes. "Be careful in there," she murmured. "Don't slip on the soap."

He laughed as he padded across the floor. In her bathtub he stood like a stranger amidst a bewildering array of conditioners, body mists and decorative bath soaps. She's got more of a variety of stuff in her bathroom than I have in my refrigerator. He grinned.

He showered more quickly than usual, taking probably less time than someone with two hands would have. She smiled sleepily when he returned. "Are you coming back to bed?"

"Actually, I'm supposed to go to work," he said. "I know it's Sunday, but —"

"Tell you what," she said. "I'll go take my shower, and then we'll talk about it." Her lips curved into a mysterious smile.

He smiled back. "You do that."

It seemed like she stayed a long time in the shower; he had put the shirt and tie on before she returned, and was combing his hair. She'd wrapped a blue towel around her, so that only her shoulders, and the pale, slightly freckled top of her bosom remained visible.

"You're already dressed." She sounded disappointed.

He feigned naïvete, although the shadow of a smile played on his face. "Yeah?"

"Well, we'll just have to fix that." She pulled him toward her, her tangle of wet hair sweet-smelling against his face. "I want a kiss."

He kissed her almost reluctantly, wary in spite of himself of getting the tie wet. His hand touched the towel at the small of her back, and as he breathed in her flowery scent like some opiate, he felt himself hardening against her skin, and his pulse bounded loudly into his ears. "My God," he said softly. She began to undress him, first loosening the tie, then untucking his shirt. She kissed his neck, her fingernails dragging along the wings of his shoulders. He rolled his head back, swung back to her again, kissing her wet hair, the taste of it like a flower's nectar against his lips. She sighed, long and slow, and worked her way down his torso as she had once before, long ago, kissing his belly, hips, nipples, and when she rose, he drew her tongue into his mouth, pushing against her as he tore the towel away and drew his hand away from her shoulders, slowly massaging his fingers into the nape of her neck, rolling her nipples between his thumb and forefingers. She felt a shock of pleasure that went all the way to the soles of her feet, and pushed against him, her breasts covering his chest. He pressed his palm against her thighs, swimming in an immeasurable sea of pleasure, floating, his pulse in his ears pounding. Oh God, he said to himself. It seemed impossible he should be here in her apartment, her bed, with his shirt hanging loosely around him and his tie knotted loosely getting twisted between them. It did not matter, nothing mattered now but the silence creating itself around them, a silence in which moved only a series of rudimentary sounds—exhalations and rustles, the hum of blood in their ears, little exclamations of delight that escaped from Maria's lips, it was as if they were creating the only noises that existed, surrounded by a globe of measureless quiet. He ran his fingers lightly around the curve of the hip that was like the shape of a violin, and her body seemed almost to leap up in response to his every gesture, her lips hot against the nerves of his neck, he felt a tremendous tingling there that was not like being tickled, but better, the caress of a silken breeze, or a burst of enveloping warmth when emerging from darkness onto a summer afternoon.

And he began the slow ascent of the curves of her body, touching her nearly everywhere, yet avoiding with an almost studious care the soft down of her sex, he worked his way up to find her breath coming out now in a long and seemingly agonized suspiration, and she was surprised to find him now avoiding her mouth, too, and although his eyes were closed she could see from the corners of his lips that he knew what he was doing, and why. She sought his lips with hers, hungrily, and he grazed them for just an instant but continued to kiss the cheeks and chin, the forehead like pale moonlight glimpsed between trees, and down he went against her breast, her skin salty and scented faintly, a lingering scent of lilacs, he moved with a kind of rhythmic power and grace, so that to her the feeling was like that of attack and retreat, where he would kiss, lick, bite, and then, retreating, glide the fingertips or tongue down to the next surprising place, never passing within the periphery of the insides of her silken thighs, and she began to grow frantic, urgent, pushing against him, trying to satisfy the desire rising within her by rubbing herself around his leg, and yet he held her back, not letting her, it was not time, and in the heat and growing wetness between them she felt only an incredible electricity, gone were the warmth and glow of the previous moment, she was crying out for him now, and as the soft guttural sound of her passion began to escape from her throat, he was surprised to find that she had not only moved fully beneath him, she had forced herself up against him, her back arched, in a way that made delay no longer possible, and she was grasping his back and buttocks with her fingers, frenzied, biting into the silk tie around his neck, and even in that frenzy she was beautiful, beautiful like sunlight scattered on the petals of tulips, and when he entered her she drew her breath in sharply, throwing her legs around him, her head back, eyes closed, lips slightly parted, he slowed, touching the delicate mouth with his fingertips, looking down into her deep eyes as the fragrance of her filled the room, he was nearly weeping with joy, and could only say, "I love you," before their lips met.

Afterward, they lay for a long time together, coasting on the wave of quiet contentment that sustained them. They spent that day together—he took a one-day reprieve from work—and for the first time since winter, they went walking together in Bruford Park. Slowly they walked among pines and sycamores, talking quietly, an occasional laugh breaking from one or the other.

She told him, in her quiet way, that she could not fix his problems. The difficulties of his accident, emotional and otherwise, were things he would need to work out for himself. But she assured him that she was more than just his friend, and that they could indeed talk about anything together from that day forward. He only smiled, squeezing her hand slightly in response. The trees above them were high and green, the sky like a stained glass window, and they walked slowly on beneath the sun.

CHAPTER FORTY-SEVEN

SOMETIMES IT WAS difficult for Johnny Caruso to see clearly.

Slumped back in the seat of the Camaro and listening to a song he did not like at all, he wanted to change it, but he was almost comfortable, and besides, the radio seemed a long way away. He traced circles in the air with a cigarette, watching the little arcs of light imprinted on the night. When he finished the cigarette and stubbed it out in the tray, he struggled forward and changed the station. A song came on that he hadn't heard in a long time, and he repeated the lyrics as it blared:

That's the place that's better,
Where I can just forget her
And let the wound heal.

He looked down on Carverville for the last time.

"I'm gonna blow this clambake," he said aloud. "This town is history for me."

When the police found his body the next morning, he would look like someone who had not planned to leave town or this world: his eyes would be closed, his mouth open a crack, like a door slightly ajar. For now, his eyes were wide open, and he popped another Nembutal into the mouth that would soon be scrutinized by police, chasing it down with more Scotch.

The song ended, and "Sympathy for the Devil" came on. It had always sounded powerful and defiant, but now, in the slowing and sinking of all that surrounded him, it cut him to the quick.

He pressed the radio's black button dramatically and switched to another station—"*...but I never said goodbye*" screamed out of the speaker and he turned the black dial slowly to the left until it clicked. Only the sound of crickets remained in the wavering darkness.

He tried to think about his life, tried to focus on where he'd been, what he'd done, where he was heading. He struggled, remembering he was not loved, and that he'd had to bear a heavy load. He did not remember what, exactly, he'd ever done wrong. He knew only that he'd hurt and been hurt and that these thoughts, swirling around in his head in a many-voiced babbling, were too unbearable to behold. Crickets chirruped in the darkness outside the car, they sounded far away, and suddenly words like *nihilism* and *cynicism* and *existentialism* seemed utterly meaningless, replaced almost before they disappeared by the tangible sounds of *penitence, shame, regret, remorse*, and a chorus of *hows* and *whys* so profound and intractable that they receded before he could grasp their import, floating away beyond the rim of the great black emptiness opening beneath him.

WANT MORE?

I'm truly grateful to you for taking the time to read this novel. I hope it took you on a ride. It took me about seven years to complete, and is among the great accomplishments of my life.

If you'd like to read my other novels – each of which also took about seven years to complete – please visit my website at http://www.msahno.com/books. If you join my free email newsletter, you'll get news on upcoming events, along with my free e-book, Marketing for Authors.

For today's independent authors, book reviews are like currency. If you enjoyed this novel, please post a review of it on https://www.goodreads.com or https://www.amazon.com. If you email me to let me know that you've reviewed it, I'll send you a special bonus PDF of exclusive material.

Of course, if you liked the novel, I hope you'll recommend it to others and follow me on social media. You can follow me on Twitter at https://twitter.com/MikeSahno or like my Facebook page at https://www.facebook.com/sahnocomm. Thank you all.

- Mike

ACKNOWLEDGEMENTS

COUNTLESS INFLUENCES SHAPE an author's life and work, and space does not permit thank yous for all of them. But on some level or other I am gratefully indebted to the following people whether their help was inspirational, editorial, instructional, emotional, spiritual or all of the above: the lovely and wonderful Sunny Sotgaew Sahno, Bob Sahno, Evelyn Sahno, Cory Andrew, Lou Berkman, Don Booth, Geodie Baxter-Bowen, Xena Brown, Paul Bouyea, Martha Calligan, Michele Carrell, Bruce Cockburn, Janet Davidsen, Linda Rurka Dooley, Christie Bracciano, Jim Ellis, Tara Engstrom, Cha Gray, John Guzzardi, William Hanna, Lori Jewell, Gemma & Larry Kay, Tom Kelly, Mark & Elizabeth Leib, David J. Lipani, Virgil Mandanici, Joni Mitchell, Lyle & Caroline Mosier, Donna Murphy, Jennifer Nolen, Lorin Oberweger, Phil Ochs, Craig O'Neil, Angela Perkins, Fred Rezler, Liz Rosenberg, Ron Scott, Paul Stober, Sr. Marguerite Tarleton, Scott & Lauri Toler, Nick Vukasinovic, Ed Whittle, Dot Wilson, Brenda Windberg, Lisa Zackowski, Frank Zappa, Mike S., Rob D., Dick & Judy P., Brenda D., Kenny & Pat H., Ron B., Paul G., Kathi W., Eddie H. and Nancy A., the late Stan Geda and Jeremy Crowe, and above all, Mr. G.

Special credit/thanks to M.D. Fletcher, author of Contemporary Political Satire: Narrative Strategies in the Post-Modern Context, New York: University Press of America, 1987, for the phrase "… great primal joke of the undignified nature of the human body."